Sam's life changed forever

Sam Russell had never been to a horse race, so nothing had prepared him for the equine thunder that roared up the track toward him.

Horse and rider ran as one. They made the air quiver with the energy of their race.

No living thing could catch them. Sam stood up, unable to sit still. *Lynn was right,* he thought. *They are an unbeatable team.*

Now they were slowing. Sam sat down, his heart pounding in his chest as they cantered past him. She was up in the stirrups, allowing the horse to move around the track at his own pace. Lightning's coat was shiny with sweat, and the heat of his body steamed the early-morning air. At last Lynn rode up to the bleachers and reined him in.

"Well," she said to Sam. "What do you think?"

"I think..." was all he said. Something inside him exploded. All weariness faded and he wanted to jump and holler and...

...tell her he loved her?

Special thanks and acknowledgment to Sharon Brondos
for her contribution to the Crystal Creek series.

Special thanks and acknowledgment to Sutton Press Inc.
for its contribution to the concept for the Crystal Creek series.

To Tottie Ferris, a true Texas lady

Published June 1993

ISBN 0-373-82516-1

WHITE LIGHTNING

White Lightning

Sharon Brondos

Harlequin Books

TORONTO • NEW YORK • LONDON
AMSTERDAM • PARIS • SYDNEY • HAMBURG
STOCKHOLM • ATHENS • TOKYO • MILAN
MADRID • WARSAW • BUDAPEST • AUCKLAND

Dear Reader,

Welcome back to Crystal Creek! In the heart of Texas Hill Country, the McKinneys have been ranching, living and loving for generations, but the future promises changes none of these good folks could ever imagine!

Crystal Creek itself is the product of many imaginations, but the stories began to take shape when some of your favorite authors—Barbara Kaye, Margot Dalton, Bethany Campbell, Cara West, Kathy Clark and Sharon Brondos—all got together with me just outside of Austin to explore the Hill Country, and to dream up the kinds of romances such a setting would provide. For several days, we roamed the countryside, where generous Texans opened their historic homes to us, and gave us insights into their lives. We ate barbecue, we visited an ostrich farm and we mapped out our plans to give you the linked stories you love, with a true Texas flavor and all the elements you've come to expect in your romance reading: compelling, contemporary characters caught in conflicts that reflect today's dilemmas.

Lynn, the youngest of J. T. McKinney's offspring, and the heroine of Sharon Brondos's *White Lightning,* is in many ways a rebel. Not only does she stubbornly insist on raising and training a Thoroughbred in an area of the country that has little knowledge of the majestic breed, but she also manages to fall head over heels for a man whose urban, professional, paternal life-style is totally foreign to her.

Next month, in Margot Dalton's delightful *Even the Nights Are Better,* Lynn's widowed aunt Carolyn is amazed to find herself pursued from a highly unexpected quarter. Texas real estate suddenly takes on a whole new meaning....

C'mon down to Crystal Creek—home of sultry Texas drawls, smooth Texas charm and tall, sexy Texans!

Marsha Zinberg
Coordinator
Crystal Creek

A Note from the Author

During my preteen years—a long, long time ago—I read and thoroughly enjoyed girl-and-horse books. Although I rode horses in both equitation show and jump class, I never had my own horse, and the books gave me a way to fantasize about the possibility.

Now, many years later, I still have never owned a horse, but I do have my own books. In *White Lightning,* I have written a girl-and-horse—and hero—book for myself. The story of Lynn, Lightning and Sam is for all those who, as girls, dreamed of having a horse, and as women, dream of loving a winning man!

Sharon Brondos

Cast of Characters

AT THE DOUBLE C RANCH

John Travis (J.T.) McKinney	Rancher, owner of the Double C, his family's ranch. A man who knows his own mind.
Cynthia Page McKinney	J.T.'s wife. An ex-Bostonian bank executive learning to do things the Texas way.
Tyler McKinney	J.T.'s eldest son, a graduate of Rice University. Now he wants to grow grapes in his daddy's pasture.
Cal McKinney	J.T.'s second son, an irresistible and irrepressible rodeo cowboy.
Serena Davis	The bootmaker who turned Cal's head.
Lynn McKinney	J.T.'s only daughter. She bucks the trend by raising Thoroughbreds in quarter horse country.
Hank Travis	J.T.'s ancient grandfather. Old Hank has seen and done it all.
Ruth Holden	Californian vintner, daughter of Dan Holden, J.T.'s old army buddy. Ruth is visiting the Double C to help Tyler plan his vineyard.
Lettie Mae Reese	Cook. } Together they know all
Virginia Parks	Housekeeper. } the household secrets.
Ken Slattery	Foreman at the Double C.

AT THE CIRCLE T RANCH

Carolyn Randolph Townsend	J.T.'s sister-in-law and neighbor.
Beverly Townsend	Carolyn's daughter and a former Miss Texas.
Lori Porter	Carolyn's cousin. Lori lives at the Circle T and keeps the ranch accounts.

AT THE LONGHORN

Dottie Jones	Owner of the Longhorn Motel and Coffee Shop.
Nora Jones	Dottie's son's ex-wife.
Martin Avery	Mayor of Crystal Creek.
Bubba and Mary Gibson	Old friends of J.T.'s.
Nate Purdy	The McKinneys' family physician.
Vernon Trent	Real-estate agent.
Wayne Jackson	Sheriff.

NEWCOMERS TO CRYSTAL CREEK

| Dr. Sam Russell | An Austin dentist who's invested in Lightning but is interested in Lynn. |
| Allison and Alexandra Russell | Sam's daughters—they're becoming teenagers much to their daddy's dismay. |

CHAPTER ONE

HOOVES THUNDERED down the track as Lynn McKinney rode Lightning. They ran faster than the wind, faster than sound, faster than light itself. Faster, even, than time.

It was the race of their lives. Lynn felt a sense of urgency. It was as if everything in the universe depended on their winning the race.

They were a team. Unbeatable, unique and far more than just the sum of the two of them, woman and horse. Together, they were a champion, a winner, a force that could not be defeated. They ran to where the finish line and victory waited.

Closer, closer to the finish line...Lynn could taste the victory. But, suddenly, without warning the finish turned into a brick wall rising from the ground and looming high above them. Lynn screamed a warning to Lightning....

And woke up.

A HALF HOUR LATER, Lynn entered the warm darkness of the stable. Horsey smells, as familiar as her own scent, filled her nostrils. Leather and saddle soap wafted from the tack room. Oats and hay contributed a hearty fragrance. Beneath her boots, straw crackled and added its dry, dusty-sweet aroma to the air.

Out of the dark, from his wooden room down the line of stalls, Lightning whickered a greeting. Then his huge hooves stomped the floor. The stable shook slightly with each impact. His whinny of impatience echoed in the dark space.

"Hush, fella. You're going to wake the world," Lynn chided the big animal. "I'll be with you in just a second."

She turned into the tack room, switched on the lights and gathered up saddle and bridle for the first workout of the day. Later, she would use the proper racing tack, but now she used her own specially designed saddle and bridle—scarcely more than a soft leather pancake of a saddle seat and a modified hackamore for a halter made with the purpose of letting her stay as closely in touch with the horse as possible.

That was vitally important to her style of training. When she and Lightning finally ran in a major race, they would have to think and move as one being!

They were not ready for that at this point.

But, soon... Soon.

Lightning whinnied again, this time shrilly. He wanted her attention, *now*.

"I'm coming, Your Majesty," she called, the horse's eagerness infecting her. "Just try to have a little patience, could you?"

Patience, however, was never Lightning's best quality. He snorted again, stomped and whinnied so loudly, he sounded like a trumpet. Lynn sighed, made tsking sounds and shook her head like a mother fussing over a problem child. She knew patience was definitely the characteristic he needed the most work on. Maturity and racing experience would help. But that was for the future. For the future, *if* she could get things worked out.

No. *When* she got things worked out. Meanwhile, there was training to be done. Lots of training.

By the time she reached his stall, he was literally frothing at the mouth and shaking with eagerness like a puppy. His huge hooves beat a frantic tattoo on the floor.

"You big, old baby," she said. "Can't you wait one more second?"

He stomped again. Shook his thick black mane. *No!*

"Oh, come on, Lightning." Scolding him softly, she greeted him with an affectionate pat on his nose and gently scratched the sensitive skin by his ears. He stretched his neck and snorted again, demanding more. When she handed him the carrot, he lipped at it, delicately, then chomped, indelicately, devouring it instantly and nosing at her for more.

"Don't be such a greedy brat," she added, aware her tone of voice was too gentle to have any effect on his behavior, but unwilling to speak harshly to him. He was so much more to her than merely a professional partner. He was what no racehorse should be to his trainer.

He was her pet.

Lightning dropped his head and sighed, contented. She opened the stall door and murmured soothing sounds. The big colt pulled back, becoming calmer as he recognized the onset of the dawn ritual.

Lynn continued to speak to him as she touched him, stroking his silky black coat. "That's right, boy," she cooed. "You're big and strong and healthy, and all we have to do is make sure the right things happen for you." She was reassuring herself as much as the horse. "Yes, it's all going to be fine. Just you wait and see. I'll talk to those men, and make them understand what we have to do."

Soon he was almost purring like a large kitten. When she was satisfied with his state of mind, she slipped on the hackamore and led him out into the stable. Looping the reins around a ring, she set the small saddle on his back and cinched the girth.

Lightning whoofed as the belly strap tightened, then he shook and neighed. *Time is awasting,* he seemed to say. *Let's get on with it!*

"Okay, fella," Lynn said, slapping his muscular neck playfully. "Let's go." Then she led him out of the stable. With a lithe movement, she mounted and drew up the reins. Both she and Lightning voiced their happiness, glad shout and whinny blending in the cold dawn air.

Lynn felt a bolt of energy go through her, as if her contact with the horse gave her fresh strength and courage to go on with her dreams. She felt more like a wild young child than like the serious, twenty-five-year-old professional horsewoman she really was. And Lightning frisked like a foal, throwing up his head and making his mane wave like a long, silky black flag. Laughing, Lynn gave him the signal and he started trotting down the path toward the racecourse. Their morning was finally beginning.

They entered the ring and walked around the track a few times, giving both of them a chance to warm up for the real workout. Lynn felt him tremble beneath her and sensed that her own body was wired just as tightly. Ready to snap.

Ready to run.

After a while, she urged him into a trot, riding high—almost standing above the saddle while he worked into the gait.

Then a canter. She settled down onto the saddle, her legs bent nearly double and her knees tucked neatly close to the horse's sides. Both hands on the reins—Lightning needed no whip to goad him into running!

Finally, "Okay, boy," she whispered. "Take it away. Go for it!"

And Lightning flew. Flew around and around the track, making the earth shiver beneath him.

They ran faster than the wind, faster than sound, faster than light itself.

Lynn allowed her imagination to take over. Lightning's speed gathered momentum and he was leading the pack. People in the stands were cheering, but Lynn was only vaguely aware of them. The clattering of hooves was deafening. She and Lightning were coming to the finish line. She felt him straining and she knew nobody would beat them.

Then he stumbled. . . .

And she woke up from her daydream just in time to lean farther forward to help him steady himself. He switched leads and made up for his lost pace in a moment. Lynn felt a swell of pride at this, and a determination to allow nothing to stand in the way of Lightning becoming the champion she knew he could be.

Nothing and no one.

And that included the three Austin dentists who were now her partners. Racing and training Thoroughbreds was expensive, and Lynn needed the financial resources the three had offered when her previous partners had withdrawn. But this new alliance was barely a month old and Lynn hadn't had a chance to go over her plans with them, hadn't had a chance to establish the kind of rapport with them that she'd had with the original three. These guys hadn't even seen Lightning. But they seemed to have very definite ideas of their own, and they were putting pressure on her that she did not like.

She had to take further steps, she decided. And for that, she needed a lawyer, one whose advice she could trust completely. None other than her father's old friend and the family lawyer, Martin Avery.

She finished her ride and went back to the house, determined to meet with Martin as soon as possible.

ABOUT TWO HOURS LATER, on that same cold morning, Dr. Sam Russell's day began. Wakened from a sound and dreamless sleep by the persistent alarm, the dentist fumbled for the clock and shut it off. The instant silence was a relief.

Sam stood up carefully. The room was icy. He grabbed his bathrobe and shrugged into it quickly.

He walked to the bathroom, flicked on the light and stared at his reflection in the mirror.

He did not look terrific. In fact, he looked far older than his actual thirty-five years. The graying hair along the edge of his temples had been there for some time, partly hidden by the sandy-blond color of the rest of his hair, but other signs of stress had appeared over the past few months. Stress that had left its mark in the deepened lines on his face and in dark patches under his bleary blue eyes. *Wake up, Russell,* he told himself. *The girls are depending on you.*

In a few short hours, they had a plane to catch. He turned away from the mirror. Soon they would be on their way to Chicago. On the way to making what might be a life-changing decision for one of his daughters. Maybe for both of them...since they were tied so close together emotionally.

And for himself?

Sam didn't know. All he did know was that the girls were relying on him to make the right decision. And he had to make it on his own.

"I'VE GOT a real problem, Martin," Lynn said as she set her file of documents on the lawyer's desk. "I want Lightning to race next year in the Triple Crown. I hope to have him run in the Creole Stakes next month over in Louisiana. It's an important race on the way to the Crown. As his trainer, I see him well worth the time and financial investment, and my new partners, the dentists, don't. They want to stick to small, local races where they're sure he'll bring in a steady, but modest flow of cash. That'll not only spoil him silly, making him think he can win anything, it'll sharply reduce his ultimate value as a stud."

Trying not to smile at Lynn's references to her horse's attitude and romantic future, Martin Avery nodded and opened the file in front of him. In spite of the humor of it, he did realize Lynn was talking about some very serious financial matters. He adjusted his reading glasses and scanned the first document, the contract of joint ownership, without speaking.

"I want to keep Lightning out of all races until I get some cooperation from the others. Can I do that?"

Martin pushed the contract to one side. "Possibly. Let's go over the whole situation. Just to refresh my memory." He sat back, took off his glasses and rested his elbows on the arms of his chair. He gestured for her to sit down.

Lynn took a seat in the leather chair for clients and went on with her explanation. "As you know, this partnership was formed about a month ago when the original investors sold their shares to these guys. I know I need their financial backing, but I didn't expect them to interfere with my and Lightning's agenda. They're dentists, for Pete's sake. They know nothing about racing. But they're in a hurry to get a return on their investment. If I stick to my plan and go for the Roses, the Kentucky Derby, they won't get much money for a while. But if I win, they'll eventually see millions. All I'm asking for is their patience."

Martin Avery picked up the folder containing the contract. "Well, I'll just take a look at this," he said. "But I can't make you any promises." He ran the palm of his hand over his hair and smiled sympathetically at her.

Lynn nodded. "I understand that. I only want to know if I have any legal right to decide what's best for Lightning."

"Doesn't sound like too much." Martin regarded Lynn. "Let's start at the beginning," he suggested, taking out a long yellow legal pad and scrawling some notes at the top of the first page.

"Okay." Lynn settled back in the comfortable chair. "As you know, I know quite a bit about training and racing Thoroughbred horses. I've been doing it professionally now for more than four years."

"Since you got out of college."

"That's right. And before that, I worked during the summers as a groom at the Blasedale Stables in

Kentucky and earned my silks on the small tracks in the South. But now..."

"Let me interrupt just for a second." Martin held up a hand. A look of concern shone from his blue eyes. "You've never raced in the big-stakes races?"

"No. But—"

"Don't get defensive." He smiled again. "I'm only playing devil's advocate."

"Okay." She took a deep breath. "I'm sorry. Lightning means everything to me. I saw him born. Two years ago in Kentucky. I knew his dam and sire, and had kept an eye on the mare's pregnancy. When it came time for the foal to be delivered, I made sure I was there."

"I remember. That's when you decided you wanted him?"

"Yes. And that's where the problem began. He was just too valuable. Even if he never won a race, his bloodline was tops. Enough to place a very high price tag on him. Which was why I found that group of business people in Lexington who were willing to join in a partnership with me."

"But you didn't have to put up any cash. The agreement was that you would stable and train him at the Double C, and that when he was ready to race, you would ride him. That would be your one-fourth share."

"That's right. Actually, it was a really good deal for the others, since the expense of housing and preparing him would have been almost prohibitive for them."

"What made them change their minds?"

Lynn shifted nervously in the chair. "I guess they didn't take into consideration the amount of time between the initial investment and any profits. They were all three successful Kentucky business people. I thought they understood the process and the risks, but I was mistaken."

Martin tapped the table with the tip of his pen. "I remember asking you when you came to me with this plan whether your personal enthusiasm for the animal had anything to do with swaying them to invest in the first place."

"I admit I put up a good sales pitch." Lynn looked at the lawyer with a steady gaze. "But my enthusiasm was and is well placed!"

"I'm sure it is," Martin replied, his tone sincere. "But, Lynn, you know that not everyone gets all worked up about Thoroughbreds the way you do."

Her smile was wry. "Especially not around here."

"And this new bunch of investors are Texas folks, aren't they?"

"Yes." Lynn picked at the arm of her chair with a blunt fingernail. "Three dentists from Austin. I asked the first group to try selling their shares to people around here, since I was stabling and training Lightning out at the ranch, and wanted folks who could come out and watch him in action. One of the dentists has a financial adviser who knew one of the people in the original group and—"

"Lynn, why didn't you discuss this new agreement with me?"

"I honestly didn't think it was necessary. I was sure these new people would want the same terms as the others. They would leave the training to me. But now it seems they are determined to make some speedy money."

"Nothing wrong with that, as long as it's legal," Martin said.

"Of course not. But the point I'm trying to make is that it would be a waste to run Lightning in the small-time races. He should be running the Kentucky Derby next year!"

"And if he does?"

"If he does and *when* he wins, he'll be worth not thousands, but millions." She gestured widely. "All a horse has to do is make a good showing in that race and his stud fee becomes enormous. I know that if I'm allowed to bring Lightning along my way, he will win. And then the sky's the limit."

Martin looked more interested. "And have you explained this to the other three people?"

She settled back, the excitement gone from her face. "I tried. With two of them I hit a brick wall. All they want is instant money. They seem to think of horses like something in the stock market—all paper, no reality."

"And the other guy?"

"I haven't met with him yet. I've tried to see him, but he's always busy. I called this morning again but he's out of town. In Chicago, I was told. Something to do with his family. He's a widower with two little children, so I'll have to work around his schedule."

Martin frowned. "Maybe he doesn't want to discuss it."

"Maybe. But until I hear it from his lips or see it in writing, I won't give up." She sat forward again. "I can't, Martin. This horse is my one big chance. I *know* it. If I can take him as far as I know he can go, I'll be able to build my professional career around him." She paused. "My whole future, in fact."

Martin Avery nodded slowly, studying the young woman sitting in front of him. He'd known her since the day she was born. The only girl child in the McKinney family, she'd come into the world with the feisty attitude necessary for survival in a male-dominated household. Her petite size belied her inner strength. Martin had come to respect the professional ability, determination and business acumen she had shown when she had decided to become a professional jockey and trainer. And she knew the racing business well. If she said this horse of hers could win fame and fortune, it was quite likely he could.

Martin wanted to help the young woman. "All right," he said. "Let me spend some time checking these documents, and I'll let you know what I think. Sounds to me like you ought to keep after that third man, however. Call him and make him talk to you. Make him listen. If you can get him to agree with your plans, you'll be further ahead. Fifty percent of a partnership is far better leverage in deal making than twenty-five percent."

"I know." Lynn stood up. She held out her hand. "Thanks, Martin. I'll wait to hear from you."

They shook hands. "Right," the lawyer replied. "Give your daddy and Cynthia my best regards."

"I will. Thanks again."

Lynn left the law office and went outside. The discussion with Martin had been encouraging and she felt more cheerful and optimistic than she'd been for weeks. The town of Crystal Creek seemed to embrace her like a friendly relative.

She decided to go to the Longhorn for pie and coffee.

The coffee shop was quite busy. Half a dozen folks greeted Lynn and she smiled in response. The local veterinarian, Manny Hernandez, insisted she join him and Sheriff Wayne Jackson.

"Hey there, little McKinney," the sheriff said. "What brings you into town today?"

"I thought you didn't leave the ranch anymore until you'd tucked that big old horse of yours into his stall for the night," Manny added, teasing. The handsome veterinarian and Lynn were good friends, although at first when Manny set up practice in the county, he'd seemed to think their mutual love of horses might lead to something between them. It hadn't happened, but their friendship had strengthened over the years.

"Good morning to you, too, Manny." Lynn grinned at the two men and nodded to Dottie Jones, when the owner of the café asked whether she wanted pie and coffee. "Thanks Dottie. Sounds great. Morning, Wayne," she said to the sheriff as she sat down. Then, in response to Manny's question, she added, "I made an exception today. I had to see Martin about some business."

Manny's teasing expression faded. "Trouble?"

"Um-hmm," Lynn said, noting that both men looked interested and sympathetic. She smiled at Dottie as the pie and coffee were set in front of her, then said, "Let me tell you all about it."

The two men listened intently as Lynn talked.

CHAPTER TWO

"OPEN WIDE."

"Ahhhhrrr."

"A little wider." Sam Russell inserted the dental mirror carefully into the patient's mouth. "That's good," he said soothingly. "Excellent. The replacement fillings look good. I think from now on you'll find you feel a lot better, Fred."

Fred Adams closed his eyes and the corners of his mouth turned up in a relieved smile.

Later, when the last of his patients had left for the day, Sam went into his office, stared at the wall of family pictures there and massaged the sore spot at the back of his neck.

"Doctor?"

Sam looked up. Tennie Williams, his technician-receptionist, self-appointed guardian of his privacy, stood in the doorway. "Yes, Ten," he replied. "What is it?"

"Dr. Sam, I do hate to bother you right now, but do you remember a Ms. McKinney who—"

"McKinney?" The name rang a bell. "A patient?"

"No, sir. She's that horse person, Doctor."

"Oh!" he said, remembering. "Lynn McKinney?"

"Yes, sir. She's on the phone right now."

"Oh."

"Line three." Tennie waited a moment, then left the office, closing the door firmly behind her.

Sam punched the button. "Ms. McKinney, this is Dr. Russell. I—"

That was as far as he got. The woman on the other end of the line wasn't listening to anyone but herself. Sam held the receiver away from his ear and waited.

And caught something of what was being said.

"Dr. Russell, your colleagues—and my partners in the ownership of the racehorse—had the nerve to fire me yesterday. Fire me!" The woman's voice indicated she was on the verge of hysteria.

"Ms. McKinney," he said, when the wire was finally silent. "I haven't spoken to Phil or Dan, but as far as I'm concerned, they can't just fire you."

"My name is Lynn." The woman's voice still steamed with anger, but she sounded less angry. "Just plain Lynn. And my lawyer, Mr. Martin Avery, says they *can* fire me as jockey and trainer. If you agree with them, that is. And if the three of you buy me out at a fair market price. Until you do, everything is up in the air. I've slated Lightning for a race in late March, the Creole Stakes, and I intend to continue training him for it. But until I get straight with you people, he can't actually race. Please, Dr. Russell, we need to meet and talk about this."

Sam hesitated. She certainly sounded reasonable now. His problem was he had no idea what Phil and Dan were up to. And the rest of his day and evening were tied up with the girls' activities. Lynn McKinney and her problem would just have to wait.

"Ms. McKinney," he began. "I'm sorry, but—"

"I said I'll adjust to your plans and schedule. I meant it."

"Well, I..." She did sound sweet now, and sort of desperate.

"Please."

Sam closed his tired eyes and rubbed his forehead, then moved his hand around to the back of his neck once more. He sighed, knowing he'd give in. He could no more resist a quietly pleading female than fly to the moon. The girls had him well trained!

"Okay, listen," he said. "Alexandra has a music lesson at seven." He gave her the address. "Why don't you meet me there. We can talk while she has her class."

"Great! I'll be there." There was a pause, then: "Alexandra? Is she one of your kids?"

"The younger." Sam smiled. "We call…I call her Sandy, most of the time. Alexandra's kind of a long handle to put on a kid as small as she is."

A warm chuckle. "I understand smallness. I'm not a woman jockey because I'm six-foot, Dr. Russell."

"Sam, please. So I'm to look for a short woman, am I?"

"Four-ten. In heels. And I have brownish hair."

"I get the picture." Sam closed his eyes again. A short young woman. Athletic. Wiry. Probably a bit tough. Skin tanned and already weathered from exposure to sun and wind. "I'll see you tonight," he added.

"All right! Thanks."

Sam hung up, suddenly thinking that he shouldn't have agreed to the meeting until he'd had a chance to talk to Phil and Dan. In order to make any sense of what was going on, he ought to know in the first place why they had seen fit to fire the woman. He put his hand on the phone again, considering.

No. He'd just hear her out. He'd made no promises. They were going to get together on neutral ground, and he had no obligation to her whatsoever. Tomorrow or the day after, he'd call the others and get their side of the story. For now, he needed to get out of the office and home to his kids.

LYNN McKINNEY could still feel the tension in her stomach as she hung up the phone in her daddy's office at the Double C Ranch, but she ignored the discomfort for the moment. She'd made the call, actually gotten the man on the phone, and now they were all set to meet and talk tonight.

Good work, girl, she congratulated herself. *Step one, done.*

"Get him?" Her big brother, Tyler, came into the room, his arms full of books on chemistry and wine making. Tyler and his fiancée, Ruth Holden, had made tremendous headway on their winery. In the few weeks since they'd declared their love and intention to marry eventually, their commitment to Tyler's dream of having his own vineyard right on the ranch was already showing results. Now, Tyler was up to his eyeballs in planting and testing. "You look happy," he added.

"I am. After I declared I wouldn't race unless the dentists went along with my strategy for Lightning, and the two of them sent me the letter saying I was fired, I knew my only chance was to get to this one and talk him into seeing things my way. The other two are impossible. They won't listen to reason. This one, at least, sounds nice. But I bet he's bald and has cold hands and these teeny little eyes that make you feel all creepy...."

"Who's this you're talking about?" Ruth came into the room. She carried more books, and a computer printout covered with chemistry symbols and math equations.

"Lynn finally got the other dentist to see her," Tyler said, holding out his arm. "Come on over and let's see the news for today."

Ruth handed him the printout. She turned to Lynn. "So you talked to him? The one holdout on firing you?"

Lynn nodded. "I didn't get into specifics on the phone. You know I prefer face-to-face. At least he's decent enough to make time in his family life to talk to me." She explained about the child's music lesson.

"Sounds like he might be a nice guy," Ruth commented. "Any man who takes his kid to her lesson instead of sending a nanny can't be all bad. Right?"

"Right." Lynn considered a moment. "It's a good sign. Maybe he'll be easy to deal with."

"Don't ever count your grapes before harvest," Ruth teased. "But good luck."

"Thanks. I'm liable to need it, nice guy or not."

They chatted a while longer, then Lynn left the office and headed outside. The late-afternoon sunlight was warm on her face, and even though it was still February, the promise of spring was in the soft breeze.

Spring...

May. The Kentucky Derby next year...

Which Lightning should run, darn it all! With her
aboard! She clenched her small fists and marched
across the yard. Out of the corner of her eye, she saw
her great-grandpa sitting out on his front porch. He
was feeling better these days, and he waved at her,
but she just lifted a hand in reply. She was in no
mood to talk to anyone who'd dash her hopes.

Grandpa Hank tended to do that where Lightning
was concerned. He wanted her off that horse, married and getting down to the job of giving him great-
great-grandchildren.

She turned the corner of the yard to take the long
way round to the stables. It was quite a long walk,
but she needed the stretching to ease the tension that
was still within her.

"Hey, Miss McKinney." Bucky, one of the cowhands, greeted her from across a corral fence.
"Gonna take Ol' Fireball out this afternoon?"

"No, Bucky." Lynn smiled. "I've just come calling, that's all. We had our run and workout this
morning, as usual."

Bucky nodded, spit some tobacco juice and went
back to work on the mare he was training. Lynn
watched for a moment, admiring the small horse's
quick, neat movements.

Lightning was far too big to pirouette on a dime like that. Not one of the cowboys thought Lightning was worth a handful of oats compared to the highly skilled quarter horses that raced in the state on a regular basis. He was too big, too temperamental and too expensive. Thoroughbreds were just not popular here.

Yet.

She entered the stables, pausing for a moment to smell the familiar things. Hay, oats, horses...

Lightning stuck his big, long black neck out of his stall and whickered at her. Then, when she didn't move to him fast enough for his liking, he stomped his huge hooves on the floor, demanding her attention.

Lynn waited a moment. A fat mama barn cat bounced up to her feet and figure-eighted her warm, furry body around Lynn's ankles, purring for a scratching. Two kittens followed, but showed more caution. From his stall, Lightning watched, settled down, blowing air through his big nostrils.

"Hey, girl," Lynn said softly as she bent down to pet the cat. Then she went over to her favorite. He lowered his immense head and butted at her with his nose.

"You want to race again, don't you?" Lynn said, stroking his forehead and scratching the sensitive places behind his ears. Lightning snorted, impatient.

"I know," she said. "I'm working on it. Just you wait and see!"

SAM LISTENED to his younger daughter chatting away as they drove through the quiet Austin suburb where her music teacher lived. Sandy was on a roll this evening, discussing classmates, school, teachers, clothes and a whole lot of other topics that he had some difficulty following. He heard her mention something about Texas accents, but he let it pass.

"Daddy." Allie spoke up from her nest in the back seat. "You missed the turn."

"Huh?" Sam jerked out of his introspective reverie to see the turnoff to Professor Bailey's home slide by on the right. "Oh, heck, I did, didn't I." He put on the brakes and backed to the corner.

"You shouldn't do that," Allie commented. "If you miss your turn, keep on going until you can safely execute a proper solution to the situation." She said the last in a singsong voice as if she were reciting a lesson.

"Where'd you pick up that bit of wisdom?" her father asked as he stopped again to make the turn. "Sounds like you've been reading a driver's test booklet." Which, of course, was ridiculous. His Allie was only eleven. Five long years before she would be allowed even to *think* about driving.

"Jamie's brother." Sandy supplied the answer. "Clemmie."

"Shut up," Allie said, her tone threatening.

"Hey!" Sam slowed. They were nearing Professor Bailey's house. "What about Jamie's brother? Who's Clemmie? And don't talk that way to your sister, Allie."

"Nothing. Sorry." Sullenness from the back now.

Sam slowed some more.

"Are not." Sandy turned around inside the confines of her seat belt and taunted her older sister. "You just don't wanna tell Daddy about Jamie's big brother, do you. His name is Clem, but you like him, anyway. What a dumb name. I think—"

"Shut up!"

Sam stopped the car. "Okay, girls. What's going on that I don't know about?"

"Nothing."

"Daddy, she likes Clem Sears."

"Do not!"

"Do, too. You told me last night you think he's cute! So there!"

"You . . . you snitch!"

"Girls!" Sam felt a sudden sense of panic. Allie thought some boy was *cute?* The child was only eleven. He turned around and stared at his elder daughter.

The streetlight was soft and peach colored, and Allie's reddish-brown hair shone. The childish lines of her face were deepened and matured by the shadows. Her blue eyes stared back at him with a petulant defiance that had nothing of a small girl in their depths. A young woman glared out of that little face at him. She looked a trace like her mother, Marta, and even more like *his* mom, Della Russell, a Creole beauty and supposedly the pride of New Orleans in her youth. Allie was the spitting image of her late grandma.

Oh, my God! he thought. *I'm not ready for this.*

"Look," he said, his voice much, much calmer than he thought it would be. "Let's call a truce, okay? Allie, you're right. I disobeyed a traffic rule back there. And Sandy, when your sister tells you something about her feelings, you shouldn't use it to tease her. But Allison, don't you talk to either of us in that tone again. Understand me, young lady? *Both* of you young ladies?"

"Yes, Daddy."

"Okay, Daddy."

"Sorry?"

"Sorry..."

"Sorry, but..."

Sam pulled into the driveway of the Bailey mansion. The professor was wealthy—his grandfather had discovered oil many decades ago, his father had made wise investments and so Whit Bailey was able to pursue his passion of music without worrying much about his financial situation, even in hard times. "Here we are." Sam shut off the engine. "Allie, do you have your schoolwork, or something to read?"

"Sure. Why?"

"Someone's meeting me here tonight, and I have to talk some business. So we can't play cards, okay?"

"Okay."

They all got out, Sam helping Sandy with her cello and Allie taking care of herself. Her voice had still sounded sullen in spite of the apology, he thought, as his oldest trudged up the front walk to the house. She reached over and rang the bell without looking.

Reached over. Not up. Sam did some quick mental calculation. How many inches *had* the kid grown this year already?

Dr. Bailey's maid, Delores Petrie, opened the door. "Good evening, Doctor, girls," she said in her rich, mezzo voice. "And how are we all this lovely evening?"

"Fine." Allie brushed past Mrs. Petrie, barely looking at the woman.

"Okay," said Sandy.

"Hello, Dee," Sam said.

Dee raised a black eyebrow, but her dark face showed no other expression. She let them in and shut the door behind them.

Sam turned. "I'm expecting someone else, Dee," he said. "A young woman. A Ms...."

"A young lady?" Dee folded her hands in front of her. "You courting, Dr. Sam?"

"No!" Sam felt himself redden. Noted that both girls had stopped and were staring at him. "She's just a business...I mean...she's..."

"Ho!" Professor Whitney Bailey emerged from his music room, his arms spread wide to enclose all the Russells in his embrace. "Here you are, my musical family!"

"Hi, Whit," Sam said, abandoning the formality he usually used in front of the girls.

"Hello, Professor Bailey," the girls chorused, smiling now, their moods and their father's business with an unknown female forgotten. Whit Bailey was like a slender version of Santa Claus with his hearty way and his white mane of hair and beard. But he was also an exacting professional musician, successful and world-famous.

And devoted above all else to encouraging musical prodigies such as nine-year-old Alexandra Russell.

LYNN MCKINNEY PULLED UP in the driveway of the big house and parked her old green Volkswagen behind the new red Subaru with the license plate that spelled out TEETH. That had to be Russell's car, so this had to be the place.

Hmmm. Music lesson in a mansion? Something was familiar about the place, but she just couldn't bring it to mind.

She got out of her car, straightened her skirt, adjusted her jacket and strode up the walk. She rang the bell.

Because Dee was in the kitchen getting some refreshments for Allie and himself, Sam volunteered to get the door. He strode across the Spanish-tiled foyer, opened the big front door and...

"Hi," Lynn McKinney said, suddenly unsure of herself. The very attractive man at the door hardly looked like anyone she expected to meet tonight. "Is this, um...?" She looked at a scrap of paper and read off an address. "I'm supposed to meet a Dr. Sam Russell at this place, but..."

"That's me," Sam said. "I'm him. I mean, are *you* Ms. McKinney?" He seemed as flustered as she, forgetting she had told him to use her first name.

"Yes."

He stared at her. Lynn McKinney, Sam Russell realized, was no rope-and-bone lady jock. She was a delicate, petite young woman. Exquisitely groomed and elegantly dressed in a light gray business suit that emphasized her curves and showed off her shapely legs. He found himself gazing at them to the point of being really rude. Changing view, he found the rest of her just as admirable. Her face was heart-shaped, tapering to a firm chin and jawline. Her hair was not merely plain brown, but a rich auburn, and the thick weight of it swung down to kiss her square shoulders in a neat pageboy style. And her eyes...

Her eyes were like soft amber, flecked with pure gold. He was sinking into them.

Lynn looked at him. Sam Russell wasn't bald and squinty-eyed, or even remotely creepy, she thought. In fact, his hair was thick and sandy-blond, and his eyes...

His eyes were a compelling blue-gray, warm in spite of the cool color, and gave him a trustworthy appearance. He was tall, but not too tall. Not a towering six feet plus like her father and brothers, so that she had to lean back to look at them—just a good head over her. And his frame was lean and trim. Square shouldered and narrow hipped. Small worry lines cut into his forehead and between his eyebrows, but the lines around his mouth indicated he smiled more than he frowned, she decided.

She liked him immediately.

She found her voice. "I'm sorry, Doctor, but I got confused about the house. I have this strange feeling I've been here..."

She broke off the chatter. A girl appeared beside the man. Lynn could see the father in the child, but the latter's hair was darker as were her eyes. And they were fixed on Lynn with a solemn expression.

"Did you come here for lessons?" the girl asked, clearly having overheard Lynn's comment. "Were you also some kind of music genius?"

"I sure wasn't. I had trouble hitting middle C without a road map."

The girl looked at her for a moment, then laughed. Her whole face lightened and looked younger. "Good! That's funny," she declared. "Daddy, are you just going to stand there with the door wide open? Bugs might get in. Mrs. Findley's always fussing at us about that sort of thing, you know."

Sam came to himself then. He stepped aside and gestured for Lynn to enter. "Sorry," he said. "I seem to have forgotten my manners. I don't normally answer the door at Professor Bailey's home. I..."

"Oh, of course! This is Professor Whit Bailey's place. I used to visit here with my mother."

"Did you have lessons with him, ma'am?" The child repeated her question. Lynn noted that the girl was regarding her with a speculative expression.

"No. But... I know him. He and my mother were good friends a long time ago, particularly when she was on the symphony board. I doubt if he remembers me, but I sure recall him. He's a great conductor, a famous musician."

"So's my little sister. At least, she's gonna be someday." The child shrugged. "At least, that's what everybody says."

"So you have a sister?" Lynn addressed the girl directly, ignoring the handsome father. "I don't. I've got a girl cousin I'm real close friends with, but I don't live with her. All I've got around the house are two big brothers."

"I wish I had a brother." The child looked at her father. He didn't comment. He actually seemed to be having some trouble speaking at the moment, so Lynn took the initiative.

"I'm Lynn McKinney." Lynn held out her right hand to the girl, shifting the briefcase she carried to her left. "Who are you?"

"Allison Russell." Allie shook the lady's hand, thinking that this grown-up wasn't a whole lot taller than she was. That was nice, for a change. It made her feel older and more sure of herself. "Allie," she added, smiling. "I guess you don't have a nickname. Not with Lynn for a name."

"Hi, Allie," Lynn said. "No, I don't have a real nickname like you, but one of my brothers does call me Skunk sometimes."

They both giggled.

Sam said nothing. He just watched. Since her mother's death, Allie had been shy or defensive with women and now here she was, actually talking to Lynn as if they were equals or comrades in some enterprise.

"Well, hello." Dee entered the room. "You must be the young lady come to call on Dr. Sam."

Since she didn't remember the woman from her childhood visits, Lynn introduced herself, then declined an invitation to share the refreshments Dee carried on a large tray. "I really did come here to discuss some serious business with Dr. Russell." She looked at Sam. "If you don't mind, I'd like to get right to it."

"What kind of business?" Allie asked, looking first at Lynn, then at her father.

"Nothing interesting, Al—" Sam began.

"Your daddy owns part of my racehorse," Lynn said. "I need to talk to him about what's going on with—"

"A racehorse, Dr. Sam?" Dee's brows rose. "You can't be serious."

"Um." Sam came out of his thoughtful mood. "Look. It would take a lot of explaining, Dee. And we just don't have the time right now. Allie, why don't you and Dee go into the den and have a snack. Ms. McKinney and I will go..." He looked around. This was, after all, not his house.

"You two go on in the den," Dee suggested. "Allie and I'll go back out to the kitchen. How 'bout some cutthroat canasta, Allie?"

"No." Allie grinned. "Poker."

"I ain't playing poker with you, child." Dee turned her back and started off to the kitchen, snack tray still held at her midsection. "You're just too good." As Allie followed, laughing, the woman continued to mutter about young cardsharps.

"My daughter's a math whiz," Sam explained. "She also has an incredible memory. In a card game, she seems to know just what to play. And she *does* know exactly what has been played. She can wipe out an opponent in no time flat. It's downright embarrassing."

Lynn smiled. "She should take on the men's game out at the ranch. My daddy and his cowboys. Not to mention my great-grandfather! That'd give 'em something to think about. Beaten by a child, a female one at that." She grinned now, wickedly. "Can I borrow her sometime?"

Sam was enchanted. The mischief on her small face made her look scarcely older than Allie, but the lights shining in her eyes made her look...

Well, certainly not childlike!

What was his mind doing? He needed to get it back on the business at hand, or she'd really think he was strange, staring at her like that.

"Of course not," he said, hearing the stuffiness in his voice, but unable to stop himself. "My little girl playing cards with cowboys? No, ma'am." He immediately regretted his tone, even though he meant the words.

Lynn McKinney just continued to smile at him. "Spoilsport," she said softly, more to herself than to him. Then she hefted her briefcase. "Come on, then, Doctor. Let's get down to business, shall we?"

"Fine with me," he replied even more stiffly.

Lynn resisted the urge to poke him in the ribs, as she did to Tyler when he was acting all high-and-mighty like this. The man seemed to need shaking up. He was far too formal and stiff.

Don't do it, she warned herself. *Lightning's future—and mine—are in his hands.*

CHAPTER THREE

LYNN TOOK A SEAT on the comfortable, leather-covered sofa and placed her briefcase on the mahogany coffee table. "It's really a question of sports ethics in the long term. But in the short run, my immediate problem is also yours, Dr. Russell," she said.

"How's that?" he asked, sitting on the same sofa, but at a distance from her.

"Well." Lynn took out a sheet of paper. "You see, if Lightning doesn't race, you don't make any money."

He folded his hands together, long, strong-looking fingers twining nervously. "Well, of course I understood that, but—"

"And Lightning won't race as long as you people try to keep me from being on his back when he does. Riding him the way he ought to be ridden." She sat bolt upright and looked at him. "I trained him, I ride him. And, furthermore, since I also have a high financial stake in his future as well, I do have a say in what kind of race he runs. That's nonnegotiable."

Sam regarded her. Again he was struck by the similarity between her and his daughters. The defiance, the righteous anger. It was all so intense! But this was no domestic or personal dispute they were discussing here. He had sunk a considerable amount of money in that horse, and he couldn't see standing by and letting it go.

"I think I understand what you've just said," he replied, finally. "But I have to tell you that I don't understand what's led up to this moment. I didn't get a chance to call my partners and find out why they don't want you riding the animal. Why don't you tell me your side?"

"I sure as hell will...." Lynn paused. Gathered control. Chose her words. "That is, I certainly will. I have plans that run counter to yours."

Sam blinked. "Ms. McKinney, I have no plans."

"Well, then you ought to be paying a lot more attention to your business investments than you seem to be, Sam Russell. Because whether or not you know it, you've got almost criminal plans for my horse, and I tell you right here and now, I won't be a part of them and neither will my horse. That's a fact."

"I have absolutely no idea what you're talking about."

Lynn started to reply. But Allie Russell appeared at the door.

"Daddy," she said, "Professor Bailey wants to talk to you."

"Honey, tell him I—"

"It's about *Chicago.*" Allie's eyes widened. "He wants to talk to you, *now.*"

Sam sighed. "Okay. Excuse me a few minutes, will you, please," he said to Lynn.

She nodded.

He rose, seemed to gather himself for a confrontation and headed for the door with no further comment. Allie Russell stood aside and watched her father until he disappeared down the hall.

Then she looked at Lynn. "It's about this summer thing old Whit wants to send Sandy to," she said, leaning against the door frame and folding her arms. "Daddy's not sure about it, and Sandy's real upset." Her eyes seemed to shine with unshed tears. "I don't want her to go."

Lynn patted the sofa. "Want to talk about it?"

Allie hesitated, studied her a moment more, then came into the room and sat. "Yes," she said, looking down at her hands. "I think I do."

"PROFESSOR," SAM SAID, speaking formally and choosing his words with care, "I just don't know if sending Sandy off for a whole summer away from her home and family at her age is such a good idea."

"You think selfishly," Whit Bailey intoned. "You must let this child grow, Samuel. It is your duty as her father!"

"She's only nine, and I..."

"I'm ten, Daddy. Nearly, anyway."

Sam turned to his youngest child. "Baby, how do you feel about this?"

Sandy shrugged. Wouldn't meet either man's gaze directly.

"You saw the music school," Whit declared. "Your father took you there last month, and you saw, didn't you, girl?" His tone was kind, but had an edge of sternness under it.

"Yes, sir. But—"

"And did you not see children your age and even younger who are there for the entire school year? Not just the summer?"

"Yes, but—"

"And did they look happy?"

"Professor, I don't think—" Sam began.

"Answer me, child!"

"Yeah!" Sandy stood up. "They looked happy. But I won't be! They don't like me. They think I talk and dress funny. I want to stay with my Daddy! Not go off with people I don't know who don't even like me!"

"Sandy, I'm sure they liked you and you look just fine. What others think of you is not a reason to turn your back on this opportunity." Sam reached out for her, but she turned away.

"I don't want to go!" And with that, Alexandra Russell threw down her cello bow and ran from the room, sobbing loudly.

BACK IN THE DEN, Lynn felt her eyes tearing as she listened to little Allie talk about how much she missed having a mother. Lynn could identify completely with the child. And when she told Allie about Pauline dying the child had really opened up.

"Your daddy got married again?" Allie asked, considering the subject seriously. "And you didn't like it?"

"I did when he and Cynthia really did get married," Lynn corrected. "It was just when I first met her that I hated the idea of having someone else with my daddy besides my mother. I have to admit I wasn't real nice about it, either," she commented, mostly to herself. The memory of the pranks she had played on Cynthia still stung at her conscience, even though she'd long since been forgiven and the events were largely forgotten. "My real mama seemed too perfect for anyone to take her place."

Allie nodded understanding and looked at the floor. "What do you do?" she asked, deliberately changing the subject.

"I train and race Thoroughbred horses."

Allie stared. "Really?"

"I'm a jockey-trainer," Lynn explained. "I teach young horses how to win races, and then I ride on them so they can do it."

"Wow!"

Lynn laughed. "So I guess you might say I'm a mama to horses. I teach them, and..."

Another child came running into the room, her pale little face blotched with fury and wet with tears. She saw Lynn, ignored her and flung herself at the older girl. "Allie, don't let them send me away," she shrieked. "Don't let them do it!" Then she sobbed as if her heart would break.

Lynn didn't stop to think. She acted.

When Sam came back into the den, he was met by a sight that shocked him, then tore right at his heartstrings. The McKinney woman was on the floor, tailored jacket off, her shapely legs sprawled out as she held both his daughters on her lap and in her arms, hugging and comforting them. She was talking softly to the children, but the moment she saw him, she glared at him. "I don't know what's going on," she said, "but this child is heartbroken, Dr. Russell!"

Sam stumbled around for words for a second, then threw up his hands in defeat.

It beat crying or yelling. Which was what he really felt like doing.

"Say something, Daddy!" Allie wiped her eyes and imitated Lynn McKinney in her tone of voice and choice of words. "Sandy's just... just heartbroken."

"I... I'm sorry." Sam resisted the urge to laugh and sat down on the sofa, a safe distance from where the angry trio was parked on the floor.

He continued speaking, now addressing Sandy. "But, honey, you know very well I won't send you off to any place if you don't want to go. And it's certainly not forever, anyway. And not among perfect strangers. The teachers there were terrific." He moved closer and put his hand on Sandy's little shoulder. "Come on, baby," he said. "You liked that Miss Thomas, you know you did."

Sandy shrugged his touch off. "Not as much as you did," she said accusingly. "You just want me to go there so you can see her again, don't you? Just like Allie and Jamie's big brother. *I* know."

Sam gave up. He groaned and sat back against the sofa cushions.

Lynn realized she might have taken sides too quickly when she saw the fatigue and pain on the man's face. "Hey," she said briskly, patting their backs. "I don't know of any problem that can't be helped by talking about it over some ice cream sundaes." She glanced at Sam Russell. "How about it? My treat."

Sandy rubbed her eyes. "Can Daddy go, too?"

"Of course."

"Lynn McKinney?" Whit Bailey strode into the room. It was obvious from his apprehensive expression that he had waited outside until he'd heard the children stop wailing. "Pauline and J.T.'s baby girl?" He held out his arms. "Why, my goodness, what a fine young woman you've grown up to be! When Dee told me who was here to see Samuel, I couldn't believe it."

"Professor." Lynn gave herself up to the embrace and returned the greeting with a small hug. "Gosh, I guess you haven't seen me since..."

"Since well before your lovely mother passed away." Whit looked solemn. "How is your father doing?"

"He's remarried."

"Oh! Really? I hadn't heard about that."

"It was just a couple of months ago," Lynn explained. "She's from Boston."

"Ah." White eyebrows flew upward. "Boston? Another music patron?"

"You can ask her." Lynn smiled. Her mother had been a devoted patron of the Austin Symphony, and had been regularly courted at the yearly fund-raising event by Professor Bailey when he was conductor of the orchestra. While Whit didn't need money, himself, the symphony always did, and people like Pauline McKinney were greatly valued.

"And so I will," Whit Bailey declared. Then he turned his attention to Alexandra Russell. "My darling child," he said, his tone kind but slightly impatient. "I do not understand what has made you so very upset. But since you seem to be, I won't ask you to finish your lesson tonight."

"Thanks." Sandy swallowed the word.

"But, please, my dear," he continued. "Do think seriously about your future. The summer experience will mean a great deal to you someday. This talk about being the odd outsider does not make sense to me. If you don't go, you will regret the lost chance. I'm not trying to be mean, but I can assure you of that."

"Yes, sir." Sandy looked at the carpet. She dug the toe of her sneaker into the thick pile.

"Now, do go back into the music room and pack up your cello like a good girl." He frowned. "You were not right to throw down that bow like you did."

"I know." More toe area buried itself into the carpet. "I'm sorry."

"Well, of course, you're forgiven then." The professor ruffled the child's hair and smiled again.

Sandy left the room, her small shoulders bowed.

"She may just be too young, Whit," Sam said softly. "It may just be a year or so too soon."

"Nonsense!" Whit smiled broadly, his Santa side showing through the authoritarian one. "She's gifted beyond her years. She'll adjust, my boy. The great ones always do." As he spoke, Sandy returned, her cello case in her arms.

"I'm ready," she said. "Let's go."

Lynn regarded the small, dark-haired child in front of them. Sandy didn't look so great right now. She looked little and lost and afraid. And she reminded Lynn, oddly, of Lightning. Too ready, too soon. But really, not ready yet. Not for what he could do, if handled with love and concern for his welfare and with wisdom.

Suddenly, she knew she had an angle to present to Sam Russell. One he would understand! For now, she was content to stand by quietly and say nothing.

"I WANT A DOUBLE DIP raspberry sherbet," Allie declared, resting her elbows on the counter top and standing on her tiptoes.

Sandy wanted something a little less exotic. "One scoop, chocolate," she said, giving her own order after whispering it to Lynn. "And put jimmies on it," she added, after Lynn whispered back the suggestion.

"Me, too," added Allie.

"I want a hot fudge sundae," Lynn announced. She looked at Sam. "How about you?"

He smiled and shrugged. "Sounds good to me."

Lynn paid for the treats, and they walked over to an unoccupied table. "Lightning would love to have ice cream," she said as they sat down. "He's got a sweet tooth you wouldn't believe."

Sam made a face. "I don't think I'd want to be his dentist."

They were all laughing at this, when Sandy stopped and stared at her dripping chocolate cone. "Daddy, I really don't want to go way up there for the whole summer. Do I have to?"

Silence descended. Lynn waited, knowing this was none of her business. Then she saw that Sam Russell was looking at her.

Pleading for some help? She couldn't tell...

"I'm kind of curious about this summer thing," she said. "When you told me about it earlier, I didn't get it all straight." She stuck her spoon in the remains of her sundae and rested her elbow on the table. She did not look at Sam. She looked at Sandy.

"Well." The little girl put the tip of her finger into a drop of melted ice cream and doodled on the tabletop. "It's this place, see. Where kids go who really can do music."

"You mean, not just anybody can go? You have to be... selected or something?"

"Bingo," Allie said dryly. She stared off into the distance, her expression unreadable but her attitude clear. She was jealous of her little sister.

"Is it like Space Camp or one of those special computer camps where someone who does math like Allie can go?" Lynn asked.

Sam nodded. "Allie had a chance two years ago for something like that, but—"

"But I didn't want to go, either." Whatever Allie was staring at got farther off into the distance.

"Oh." Lynn felt at a loss. Were they too young to appreciate the opportunities they were being offered? How far did a parent have to go in encouraging children to reach their potential? Obviously parenting was no easy task.

"Well, girls." Sam slapped his palms on his thighs. "It is getting kind of late, and tomorrow is a school day. I think we'd better tell Miss McKinney thanks and head for our home. Okay?"

"Sure." Allie munched down the rest of her cone.

"I wanna talk some more," Sandy said. But her tone was listless and whiny.

"Maybe some other time, baby." Sam stood up. "Ms. McKinney, I..."

"Lynn, please! I can hardly buy a man a hot fudge sundae and insist he still call me Ms. McKinney, now can I?"

"Okay. Lynn." His smile was pleasant enough. She felt better.

"I know we didn't get much done about your horse tonight," he went on. "Why don't you call my office in the morning and have my receptionist, Mrs. Williams, set up an appointment."

"All right, Sam," she said. "I'll do that."

For a while after they left, Lynn sat by herself, thinking. The evening had been a weird one. First, going to Professor Bailey's place, seeing him again and discovering that Sam Russell's younger daughter rated the attention of a world-famous musician.

Sandy must be really special, she reflected, even though she acted like a regular kid when you talked to her.

Second, she hadn't accomplished much about her own problem, but had let herself get involved with Sam Russell's. She remembered sitting on the floor, holding the two girls on her lap and comforting them just as her own mama had done with her when she was small.

Oh *Lord!* That was downright bizarre! Lynn stood up, shaken by the realization of what she'd been doing. She'd stepped into a mother's role, hadn't she?

A substitute mother.

A *step*...

No, no, no, no...

She went outside and got in her car. How many times had she sworn along with her cousin Beverly never to get involved with any man who had lost his wife and had kids! She had suffered enough seeing her daddy court and claim Cynthia as his new wife. She *knew* what it felt like to have a mother's place taken by a newcomer. Even though, as Lynn was quick to remind herself, Cynthia had turned out to be a terrific person.

But it didn't change her resolve to stay away from single fathers. And, as attractive as Sam Russell might be, she was only interested in doing business with the guy.

Nothing but business!

LYNN ROSE bright and early the next day. She exercised Lightning as usual, and then, to her surprise, she was able to make an appointment set up with Sam Russell for later that morning. Good as his word, he had informed his receptionist to make every effort to accommodate Lynn. She was in a fine mood when she entered his office at eleven.

"Hello, Ms. McKinney. This way, please." The receptionist guided her down the hall and into a private office. "Would you care for some coffee or tea?" she asked, her narrow hands clasped together in front of her.

"No, thanks." Lynn looked around. "I'll just wait."

"He'll be with you shortly." The door closed.

Lynn strolled over to the wall where Sam Russell had some of his diplomas and a lot of pictures hanging. She looked at the diplomas for a second, then studied the pictures.

"I see you've discovered my family album." The door shut. She hadn't heard it open.

Lynn turned around. "This is quite a collection. I'm impressed. Why, your kids aren't even teenagers yet, and they've been all around this country."

Sam Russell shrugged. "We like to sightsee." He looked away from her. "Let's get to your business, please. I have patients."

"Okay." Lynn sat and took out her papers again. "Between the two of us, we own half of Lightning. Your partners own the other half. That means that even if I can persuade you to agree with my strategy for the future, we still have to bring one of the others to our way of thinking."

"And what is that?"

Lynn sat forward. "It's like Sandy."

He frowned. "What?"

"Just like your daughter. You see, Lightning is what we call a class horse. He has heart to spare. He's not just your basic oat-burner who runs because he's taught to. This animal runs because he *has* to. I tell you, he's a surefire Triple Crown champion, if I can just train him the way I know is best. Run him only in those races that will really challenge him. Stretch his natural abilities, which are considerable, and make him... well, make him supernatural. For a racehorse." She sat back. "He can do it. I can do it," she said. "If you let me."

Sam Russell remained very still. "What's any of that got to do with my daughter?"

"She's a champion, too. At least, that's what I figured out from what all of you were saying last night. But she's still a little child, as well. Just like Lightning. So she shouldn't be pushed too far yet. Nor should she be pushed into something that's wrong for her. Hold her until she's ready, *then* let the bit loose and..."

"Alexandra's not a horse, Ms. McKinney."

"I know that." She felt her temper rise, but sat on it. "The point I'm trying to make is that champions have to be handled with great care in order for their full potential to blossom at the right time. Make Sandy go to that music school before *she* decides to do it or let Lightning run in those little Podunk track races that pull you in a few thousand dollars a win and never let him face a challenge, and you'll lose them. Lose the great horse in the good one. Lose the musician in the young child." Lynn shut her mouth. If he couldn't see it now, she was wasting her breath.

Sam sat still for a while longer. His gaze never left her face. "Do you believe in fate, Lynn?" he asked, using her first name spontaneously at last and speaking in a soft tone.

"Well, I never much thought about it. But, no, I'd say not."

"I didn't think I did, either." He got up and walked over to the wall of pictures. "Until my wife died, life was pretty good to me. I had money, a terrific family, a good profession. I couldn't think of much else that would have made me happier. And then..."

Lynn waited.

"But now, things are different. I seem to live by the seat of my pants from one day to the next. My girls are changing right before my eyes. Last month—you might not believe this, but I almost had to drag Sandy away from that place in Chicago. She wanted to stay, then. She was enraptured! Enthralled. Cried when we had to leave. Now, she doesn't want to go. This morning, she wouldn't talk to me about it. She just pouted and sighed and picked at her breakfast." His broad shoulders seemed to sag. "In some ways, Allie is worse. She's shut me out altogether. I understand she's jealous of the attention Sandy gets, but I don't know what to do."

"But, I don't..."

"Then along you come, with your horse and your problem and your ways, and you charm my kids right out of their socks." He turned and looked at her. "How about a trade?"

"Huh?"

"A trade. You know, barter. I'm doing more and more of that these days right here in the office. Keep the IRS apprised of course, so no one gets in trouble, but I'll do a guy's teeth in trade for his giving my house a pest-control service, for instance. Or fixing my car."

"What do I have that you want?"

"You're a woman."

"Oh."

Sam reddened. "No, I don't mean it that way. I mean, I need your help with the girls. In exchange, I'll listen and try to understand what you want to do with your horse, and I'll try to bring my partners around to your way of thinking."

"But, Sam, I don't know anything about children. I can't help you. I would, if I thought I could. And not for any deal you and I might make. I really like the girls. But I just—"

"Last night, they were hanging on you like you were covered with molasses, Lynn. I've never seen them do that with any other woman since their mother died. Don't say you won't. Please."

"I just don't know."

"Lynn, I'm not asking you to work for me or be their nanny or even their buddy. Just..." He paused, turned away and stared out the window.

"Help," he said. "Help us. Help me."

CHAPTER FOUR

"YOU AGREED to *baby-sit*. He got you as a free baby-sitter." Hank Travis slammed down his open palm on the top of the big wooden dining table and glared at his great-granddaughter. Lynn glared back, but the old man saw her waver. "Do you deny it, Missy? Huh? Do you?" he asked, driving the point home. "You can't, can you?"

"I sure can, Grandpa! I'm not a nanny! Not now, not yesterday and not tomorrow." She spit the words at him, but her heart wasn't in it, he could tell.

Hank was delighted. Damn. This was great! He felt like having a good, friendly fight tonight. From the time he woke up from his nap, he'd been looking for some juicy trouble. Now he'd found it. He was feeling good!

Tyler cleared his throat and interjected a comment in a calm, reasonable voice. "But, Sis. It does sound like you're going to be doing some kiddie-wrangling for a while until you can get that dentist and his buddies to sign a new contract. That seems to be the deal you made with Russell."

"I didn't make a deal. I'm not kiddie-wrangling, and I'm not baby-sitting! I'm just . . . being with his kids."

"Same thing," Hank muttered, grinning.

"What's kiddie-wrangling?" Ruth Holden asked. A relative newcomer to the McKinney world, she was still unsure about a lot of their terminology.

Tyler explained. "It's the job assigned on a dude ranch to the hand who has to watch over the children of the guests."

"Oh."

"Usually the uselessest hand," Hank added, watching Lynn. He looked, Ruth thought, like one of the barn cats regarding a gopher, but with only amusing sport in mind.

"Grandpa, will you please get off it." Lynn stabbed at her food.

Cynthia McKinney shifted in her chair and sighed loudly. The family was gathered tonight for an increasingly rare evening meal together. As the winter days lengthened into spring, ranch activities ran later and later, leaving less time for scheduled dining. She had known this was coming, but it still bothered her to have the family rush into the house, grab food and rush back out. Tonight, she had hoped things would be different.

They weren't.

J.T. was brooding, his mind on ranch matters. Tyler was fuzzy-minded from trying to cram too much information about wine into his head. Ruth was distracted by Tyler. And Hank had come in from his house about an hour ago determined to pick a fight with someone. He had tried provoking everyone who went by, but no one had taken the bait. They were all too glad he was feeling better to get upset with him.

Until he'd started to needle Lynn. She'd bristled immediately and almost snarled at him when he kept it up for more than a few moments.

Which was highly unusual. Of all of the McKinneys, Lynn was Hank's clear favorite. They had a special relationship and tolerated each other to an extent that was sometimes astonishing.

"Lynn, are you sure this Dr. Russell's going to keep his side of the bargain with you?" Ruth asked. "It doesn't sound like he made you any promises."

"He didn't," Lynn admitted. She regarded her future sister-in-law thoughtfully. "I'm going to have to trust him, I guess."

Hank snorted.

"Well, Grandpa, he's trusting me with his kids!" Lynn flared. "And I made him no guarantees, myself. Just . . . some time."

"What does that mean?" J.T. asked. He'd been unusually silent during the course of the meal and the conversation. "I thought you were just giving him the benefit of your advice, being a young woman yourself and all."

"I guess I didn't mention it," Lynn said. "But the kids are spending the day here tomorrow."

"See, there. See? See what this young'n's doin'?" Hank looked around. "Baby-sittin'. Like I said. Has them stranger's kids comin' out here, gettin' in everybody's way. Makin' a nuisance of themselves. You ask me—"

"Honey, just what are you thinking of?" J.T.'s tone rose. "You can't keep an eye on two strange children. You never even baby-sat when you were a teenager. You've got other things to do."

"J.T.," Cynthia said softly. "I'd be glad to help her."

"Me, too," added Ruth.

Lynn smiled. Thanks, Cynthia. Thanks, Ruth. "But I want to do this myself. I like the kids. I want to get to know them better. I don't want anyone else to help or interfere." She glared at Hank. "Anyone. Understand?"

Hank snorted again. "Useless little females," he said. "What would I want to fuss around them for, anyways?"

Lynn had an idea about that, remembering Allie's supposed gift for poker playing, but she said nothing. Maybe tomorrow, Hank Travis would get a surprise from a girl child for once in his ninety-nine years.

"THINGS WERE lively tonight," Cynthia commented as she and J.T. got ready for bed.

"Hmmm." J.T. nodded. "Hank was sure loaded for bear, wasn't he?"

"And Lynn was no better." Cynthia frowned. "J.T., have you talked to anyone about this dentist? Who is he? What's he like? What kind of reputation does he have? I mean, is this guy just going to use her to amuse his kids for a while, then slap her dreams right out from under her?"

He was silent.

"Sorry." She looked away. "I know it's none of my business to—"

"No!" J.T. took her face in his hands. "That's not what I was thinking at all, darling. What I was thinking was, why hadn't I done that sooner."

"Check on the dentist?"

"On all of them. I had my mind too much on my own life, I think. I hardly noticed when Lynn told me the new owners were giving her some trouble. I'll check on them, all right. Especially this Russell." He grinned, then sobered. "And I think I'll let Tyler in on this."

Cynthia thought that was a good idea. Her husband had enough on his mind right now. Tyler

should take up some more of the slack, she believed.

SATURDAY MORNING Sam Russell woke up feeling
better and younger than he had in ages. He showered and dressed and the sense of anticipation and
excitement increased. *Like a kid on Christmas
morning,* he thought.

He woke the girls, promising waffles and bacon for
breakfast. They grumbled—Saturday was a sleep-
ing-in morning—until he reminded them they were
going to visit Lynn McKinney at her ranch and meet
her horse. The one that Daddy owned part of.

Moments later, they were in the bathroom, fighting over who got the first shower. Sam smiled. The
bickering was good-natured and normal. He went
out into the kitchen and opened the curtains over the
sink. The day poured in.

Late February in Austin could be miserable—a
reminder of how glum Texas in the winter fre-
quently could be. Or it could be like this morning—
bright and sunny, a promise that spring was not far
away. Sam opened the window. A soft breeze stirred
the white, eyelet curtains as he turned away and went
to the refrigerator to prepare for breakfast.

He had the meal on the table when the girls appeared, clean, scrubbed and fresh as the morning
themselves. They dug into the food.

"When are we going?" Allie asked around a mouthful of waffle. "To the ranch, I mean."

"Right after you two finish the dishes and your other chores," Sam said.

"Aw, Daddy, do we have to?" Sandy looked at him through her bangs. "I wanna..."

"Hush that," Sam said. "You know the rules, honey," he added, more gently.

"But, Daddy..."

The morning deteriorated as did Sam's good mood. By the time they were on the road to Crystal Creek, the three of them were barely speaking to one another. Hating this feeling of separation from his children, Sam gripped the wheel and drove grimly into the small town. There, he realized he didn't have the faintest idea how to get to the ranch. He pulled up at the only place where he saw cars and people. The sign read Longhorn Motel and Coffee Shop.

"DOTTIE, you just keep the coffee coming this morning, please," Manny Hernandez pleaded, his smile at the older woman guaranteeing him the attention he asked for. "I stayed up all last night with a mare that didn't want to give birth to a very expensive little foal. I need caffeine!"

"You got it." Dottie poured the rich, dark liquid into Manny's cup and then held up the pot, regarding the other three men questioningly.

"None for me." Martin Avery, lawyer and mayor of Crystal Creek, covered his cup with the flat of his hand. "Doc Purdy told me to cut it out." He grinned at the others. "I'm cutting down."

"Yeah." Wayne Jackson held up his cup for a refill. "Just like J.T.'s cutting out steak and eggs?"

"Must be terrible, getting to be an old man," Manny commiserated, no sympathy in his expression. "No meat, no coffee, no cigars, no booze, no lovely—"

"Careful, son." Martin grinned at Dottie. "Lady present."

"Sorry, Dottie." Manny actually reddened slightly. Dottie kidded him for a minute, then left.

Martin nodded. Manny was a good guy, really, in spite of his skirt-chasing attitude. "That's better. And just remember, the two of you, what you see me doing today, you get to do a few years down the line, so don't make fun."

"I'm not." Wayne drank his coffee. "In my line of work, you don't even count on tomorrow. So those folks that have the years under their belts seem like the lucky ones." To lighten the mood after the sheriff's somewhat gloomy words, Martin and Manny started exchanging remarks about the benefits of being an older man when it came to getting the ladies' attention.

It wasn't a subject Wayne found too interesting. So he took in more coffee and let his attention drift. Out of the corner of his eye, he noted that a stranger had entered the café. The man didn't look like trouble, though. Neat dresser. Fancy designer jeans, dark green crew sweater with the insignia on the chest, good haircut, real clean hands. A little too clean and neat for Crystal Creek. Indoor man—no tan to speak of. Looked like one of those Austin yuppies out for a drive in the country on a nice Saturday.

Wayne glanced through the plate-glass windows. Red Subaru parked out front. Two kids in the car. Yep. Just a Saturday tourist, looking for something to eat for his family.

"Well, you have to admit J.T.'s a happy man these days," Martin said, arguing with the young veterinarian. "He and his boys now have wonderful women to share their lives."

"And what about Lynn?" Manny didn't mention the conversation he and Wayne had had with Lynn a couple of days ago.

"Well, Lynn's got her problems right now," Martin said, indicating by his tone that he'd said about all he was going to on the topic. "Seems like the McKinney kids are all sticking their necks out in some kind of enterprise or risky deal," he added, well aware that his audience's curiosity would be piqued. "But Lynn especially. She's really run into some rough country."

"That racehorse of hers causing her trouble?" Wayne asked, his attention brought back to the table. "I thought she had a real winner there."

"She does," Manny said. "Lightning can run circles around any Thoroughbred I've ever seen eat track. I'm telling you that when she takes that colt out to the big time, I am putting big money on his ugly black nose! He's a champion for sure."

"Don't go spending your winnings just yet," Martin said. "She may end up in a lawsuit over that animal before too long."

"Aww." Manny leaned forward. "That's no good! She works like the devil's sister with that horse. And he's a winner, like I said. Lynn McKinney deserves success!" He was talking quite loudly now, and several people at other tables had stopped to listen.

Some, who knew whom and what he was talking about, nodded, agreeing. Lynn was a popular person in Crystal Creek, even though she'd broken with tradition by choosing to train and race Thoroughbreds instead of quarter horses. She was J.T.'s daughter and a cute young woman, and most of them had known her for years.

Only Bubba Gibson, sucking down his coffee over in a corner where he was obviously waiting for his girlfriend, Billie Jo, had a disparaging comment to make. "Lynn McKinney wants to fool with those damn high-priced, overbred oat-burners, she's asking for whatever trouble, if you ask me," he stated. "Damn horses, damn women," he added sullenly, addressing his coffee. He glanced out the window, looking for Billie's skirt to come switching down the sidewalk.

"Nobody asked you, Bubba," Manny exclaimed. "So shut up." Several other men backed Manny up, suggesting Bubba keep his opinions to himself.

Fortunately Billie Jo entered the café just then, and Bubba's attention was redirected.

Wayne brought the conversation back to Lynn. "How come a lawsuit, Martin? Lynn in any real trouble?" he asked. While he waited to hear what would undoubtedly be a long-winded, lawyer kind of answer, Wayne leaned back, his eyes half-closed.

Watching.

The newcomer yuppie had asked Nora something, charmed her into smiling a little, which wasn't too hard since he was good-looking, and Nora wasn't so damn blind these days. Then he'd made some notes on a piece of paper, but he wasn't leaving yet. Instead, he seemed to be eavesdropping on their conversation. Seemed real interested, in fact. Wayne watched him as Martin spoke, emphasizing the personal side of things, but telling as much about Lynn's

legal situation and financial predicament as the lawyer could without breaking any confidences.

From what Lynn had told them and what Martin
was saying, Wayne gathered that the three dentists
had bought out the controlling shares in Lightning
late in January just in time to bring Lynn's training
and racing plans to a screeching halt and throw a
monkey wrench into her dreams. The lawyer was
careful with his words but Wayne could picture the
three. Didn't know a hoot about horses and didn't
care. Didn't care about a nice, hardworking young
lady like Lynn. Didn't care about a thing but themselves, it seemed. Just wanted a quick investment
buck. Now Lynn was taking them all on by refusing
to race unless they agreed to her terms. And Lynn
would stick to her guns. She was fiercely independ-
ent—even her own daddy had to be careful about
offering help.

Wayne could appreciate how frustrated J.T. must
feel. So probably could most of the men in the coffee shop. For many the handling of the modern
Texas female was quite a problem. It was easier in the
olden days; women had seemed more willing to be
taken care of without making such a fuss about it all.

Wayne shook his head and forced himself to listen to Martin and Manny. The two were now back to
the topic of women. The yuppie, Wayne noticed,

waited a few moments then turned and left without saying anything or bothering anyone.

But he'd looked real upset. *Now why is that?* Sheriff Wayne Jackson wondered.

LYNN WAS in the small tack room of the stable mending a bridle when she heard the Russell girls' voices. She set aside the bridle and listened for a moment. They sounded excited.

She had left instructions at the house for the children to be sent down to the stable. But as she waited, the sounds of laughter and squeals faded. A few minutes later, she heard footsteps on the wood floor. Too heavy and too slow to be the children's.

"Good morning," said Sam Russell, sticking his head through the doorway. Somber as a funeral director. Not a glimmer of a grin on his face.

"Hi. Welcome to the Double C Ranch. Have any trouble finding your way?"

"Some. But I stopped for directions."

"Good." Lynn looked past his shoulder. "Where're the girls?"

"About four women surrounded them when we arrived and dragged them off to cookie heaven somewhere in the big house. Sent me off here to fetch you. At least, that's what one of them told me to do." He paused. "No, it's what she *ordered* me to do."

Lynn laughed. "Probably Lettie Mae Reese. You'd better be prepared, Sam. She'll stuff those kids so full of goodies, you'll never get their teeth clean again."

"Maybe that's what they need."

"She's cooked for us for as long as I've been alive. She dearly loves kids, and she will spoil them rotten, if you...if I... Say, weren't you just going to drop them off and leave?"

"That was the original plan."

"And now?"

"I changed my mind. I'd like to stay a while myself, if I may." His gray-blue eyes were regarding her closely.

"Oh, that's nice. Sure, you can stay. Why did you change your mind?"

"You do get right to it when you have a question, don't you."

"Yes. Mind?"

"No, I guess not." He rubbed the back of his neck. "Well, the answer's not exactly clear to me, so I'm not sure I can explain myself to you."

"Try."

"Okay." He looked at her again with a searching gaze.

"What is it? Why are you looking at me like that?"

"I think that perhaps I'm seeing you clearly for the first time," Sam replied.

"I guess you are," she said a little sarcastically. "I'm in my element here. Old jeans and work shirt. No makeup. My hair's a mess. My hands..." She held out her leather-stained and grubby-nailed hands. "Well, see? Not exactly a manicure to write home about."

"You work hard, don't you?"

"It's hard work, training and racing a horse." She shrugged and turned away from him. "I'm not working any harder than anyone else around here. It's just...different work."

"Show me."

He came closer and Lynn could smell him over the odors of the stable and tack room. Clean, spicy...

And attractive. She could definitely feel the attraction. This kind of thing didn't happen to her often. Actually she had little time for social considerations and even less interest. But here he was, this...this dentist, with his kids and his hold on her life through Lightning, and his smile and his gentle, masculine voice and his...

"Show me this horse," he said, touching her arm with his hand. "Show me *our* horse."

"He's over here," she said, pointing and leading the way. "He's got his own special suite down at the end. A kind of one-colt condo."

"Why call him a colt? Isn't he grown?" Sam stepped along, watching the straw-strewn floor for horse leavings, but finding none. The place was surprisingly clean.

"No. He's just a two-year-old," she explained as they walked through the stable toward Lightning's stall. "Every racehorse is considered to have been born in January of the year of his or her birth, no matter when in the spring the foal was actually dropped. Lightning is ahead of his class by a touch, since he actually *was* born in January. That makes him older, stronger and more confident than a horse born, say in late April."

"Is that fair?"

"It's the way it is."

"Hmmm."

"Anyway, Lightning is treated like a young prince. Which is what he is. When I first saw him, I knew he could be a legend. I saw him, and I had to buy him."

"You bought him? I thought—"

"Well, I had to get investors, of course. I couldn't afford a class foal like him on my own. So, as I guess you know, I got some other folks to buy in, and then, last month, they sold their shares to the three of you."

"Phil, Dan and myself."

"Exactly. And good old Phil and Dan decided they wanted to make some money right away. And that's when I—"

"Dug in your heels and refused to play their way?"

"Right. And here he is."

Sam stared at the huge black head and neck that extended out of the stall. The animal was coal-black, so black he seemed to gleam like polished ebony or obsidian. The beast made a low, rumbling sound, and Lynn McKinney took his head in her hands and caressed his ears. The enormous eyes closed as if the horse were in ecstasy.

"Does he bite?" Sam asked.

"Not me." Lynn stroked Lightning's neck. "But I wouldn't recommend anyone he doesn't know go rushing up to him. Especially if he thinks they're hostile. He's very protective of me, too. You'd better take it easy until he gets to know you better."

"Don't worry! I have no intention of trying to get to be good buddies with something that weighs... What does he weigh, anyhow?"

"Around a thousand pounds. He's big for his age. He's a big horse by any standards. By the time he's through racing and put out to stud, he's liable to be closer to twelve or even fifteen hundred."

"Good Lord. What does it cost to feed him?"

She smiled. "Lots. And so you can see another reason why I need investors to help out. But he's worth every penny."

Sam watched her coo over and cuddle the animal, treating him like a favored child rather than an investment. Clearly, emotional issues were involved here. He wasn't going to get the whole picture from her. She was too bound up in this creature to make entirely rational decisions.

Too bad. He had thought she was more sensible.

"You think I'm being silly right now, don't you?" she asked, turning to him and reading his mind. "All this fuss over a horse."

Sam had the grace to feel embarrassed. "Well, I... Let's just say I'm sort of..."

"Listen to me, Sam." She gave the horse another pat on the nose and stepped back from the stall. The nose followed her, and the horse made protesting noises when contact was broken. "This is not a car, a machine you can tune up just before a race and expect it to perform at its peak every time, as long as every nut and bolt are in place. This is a living being with emotional needs and feelings just like you or me. Just like Allie and Sandy."

"I don't see the connection, but if you say so..."

She moved back to the horse and gave the area behind his ears a good scratching. The animal seemed to sigh, delighted. "In most pro stables, this job would be done by a groom. Someone who takes all the time in the world with each horse, helping convince them that they're the greatest racehorses in the history of the sport. Giving their egos the training they need! Speak to any sports psychologist—they'll tell you that an athlete's frame of mind is just as important as his or her physical condition." She moved her hand down the thick neck. "Here, all that work is done by me. I'm psychologist, trainer, groom, jockey. You name it. And Lightning won't try his hardest for any other person."

"You've managed to make yourself indispensable." He had stepped back and was leaning against the wall with his arms folded. "That was smart."

"I knew I had one chance for real success in this business," she said. "And this colt was it. Not only was his breeding background remarkable, you could see in his eyes that he was a winner from the minute he first drew breath. Now, I couldn't afford to set up a whole stable system for Thoroughbreds here on the ranch. Not only would Daddy not stand for it, but unless I had tons of money—much more than I could get by inviting investors in—I wouldn't be able to afford it. So, I've put all my eggs in this one big, black basket." She gave the neck an affectionate slap.

"And if it fails?"

Her shoulders sagged, and some of the gold light went out of her amber eyes. "Then, so do I."

"You surprise me," he said. "I didn't take you for a gambler."

"I'm not," Lynn replied. "I'm not."

"Sure, you are. It takes a gambler's mind to think the way you do."

She regarded him for a moment. Then, "You really don't understand. Sit down." She pointed to a bale of hay.

Sam was suddenly aware of how much at home she was in this setting. The old jeans, the tied-back hair, even the long piece of straw she was gesturing with, all served notice that this was her turf.

"I've been involved with horses all my life," she said, taking a seat on the stable floor across from him.

"I would assume that, growing up on the ranch, all of you would be."

"We are." She smiled. "Cal has his special roper, Tyler uses his favorite old cow pony, and I..."

"Race Thoroughbreds. From childhood?"

"No, of course not. But we all learned to ride as soon as we could sit up straight. I can't ever remember not riding." She looked off into the distance. "When I was about seven, my folks took me to Kentucky to visit some of their friends. I saw Thoroughbreds out in those emerald-green pastures, and that was when I knew."

"Knew what?" Sam was drawn into her story now. He could almost touch her devotion to the animals.

Lynn drew some squiggles in the dust on the floor with the end of the straw. "First, you have to understand that I am a Texan and my people have been for generations. Texans, traditionally, race only one kind of horse—quarter horses."

"So you're bucking tradition?"

"Right." She looked at him directly, and the strength of her gaze surprised him. "When I saw those animals in Kentucky, I knew right away. My destiny was to train and race Thoroughbreds. I began to dream of having a prize stallion and champion mares and perfect foals. Here. In Texas. On a place that I owned."

Sam saw the flush of emotion in her face. He pointed at the horse in the stall behind her. "He's the stallion you dreamed of."

"Yes."

"You're very sure of yourself."

"I guess I do sound that way right now." Lynn reached up and patted Lightning's nose. The horse nuzzled her fingers with his lips. "After all, I'm trying to explain things and convince you," she said. "Of course, I have my doubts. Of course, there might be problems." She glanced up at the horse.

"But not with this guy. If you let him do what he should, he will not be a problem."

"Then what is?" Sam settled back against the stable wall. "I guess I still don't understand why you can't let him run in any race. I mean, winning is winning, isn't it? It would all go on his record, wouldn't it? That way, Phil, Dan and I would be happy, and Lightning would be running. That's what you want, isn't it?"

"No." She stood and started to pace the floor of the Thoroughbred's stall. Her agitation immediately affected the horse. He backed away from the door and snorted. Sam heard heavy hooves hitting the back wall. Lynn seemed not to notice.

"I don't want him just running and winning. As I tried to tell your friends, he is not a sports car that—"

"They aren't really friends," Sam said. "Just acquaintances."

"Whatever." She folded her arms, her hands curling into fists, and she continued to pace. Tension showed in her face and throat as the muscles moved stiffly and the cords along the column of her neck stood out. The horse whinnied now and stomped the floor several times. "Anyway," she said, "the point is that Lightning is not a machine. He's more like a person than anything else I can use for an example. If you have a champion human racer, you don't let him or her continue to run against second-class runners, do you?"

"Well, I . . ."

"No, you don't!" Her passion was evident in the heightening color on her face and the flash of emotion in her eyes. Sam felt a matching stirring as he watched. Not sexual at all, but somehow still connected to desire.

Lynn spoke on. "You test that winner against the most gifted runners in the world. That way, you increase physical ability *and* motivation."

"But—"

She stopped pacing and stared at him. "But what?" Her expression challenged him.

"But how do you know this horse can be what you think he is?" Sam stood up. "Have you run him against any so-called gifted runners yet?"

"No, but—"

"Lynn, forgive me if I seem skeptical, but I just can't buy into your dream merely on your say-so. I'm a scientist. A very pragmatic sort of person. I need to be shown proof. Concrete evidence, in this case."

She shook her head. Proof? Evidence? She could show him all the evidence in the world—Lightning's family tree would speak for itself. She could show Sam photographs, documents, prizes won by his sire and dam. . . .

But would that be enough to convince the dentist? Lynn's dream—her very reason for being—depended on the answer.

CHAPTER FIVE

WHILE LYNN was lecturing Sam on the ideals and principles of racehorse training, her older brother Tyler was setting out to discover just who Sam Russell was and what his intentions toward his baby sister might be.

J.T. had asked him to run a background check on the dentist discreetly, but thoroughly. Tyler went directly to the sheriff.

"Morning, Tyler," Wayne Jackson said, rising from his chair behind his desk. "Have a seat. What can I do for you this fine day?"

The two shook hands. "I need a little advice, Wayne." Tyler took off his hat and jacket and sat down. "And a little information."

"I'll try."

"It's this dentist who bought into Lynn's racehorse. He's kinda gotten under her skin, I think."

Wayne said nothing.

"That is, he's got these two little girls, and Lynn, well, she's agreed to help him out with them. My daddy and I, well... We... Well, we're all kind of concerned about his motivation."

"Tyler, is there anything shady about this character?"

"Well, no. Not that we know of."

"If he's not doing anything illegal, then you're wasting your time coming to me. I can't do a thing for you. What you need is a private investigator."

Tyler grinned. "That's what I hoped you'd say. Daddy asked me to do this, and I'm sort of green at it. I didn't want to bother him with a lot of questions, so I thought I'd just say I could handle it and come to you."

"J.T. all right?"

"Oh, he's fine. But you know—he's got his mind on Cynthia now as well as the ranch. He's entitled to his time with her, and frankly, I'm glad he's finally doing some serious delegating of responsibility. Why, the other day, he let Ken and me put together the yearly feed estimation without hanging over us the whole time. We never saw him, in fact, and he didn't check our figures."

"That's sure a different J.T. than the one I know."

"You bet it is." Tyler smiled. "He's really enjoying life right now, and it's damn good to see."

"About the dentist..."

"About the private investigator. Just give me his name, and I'll get the ball rolling."

It was Wayne's turn to grin. "Actually, he's a she." He took a note card from a drawer and scribbled a name and telephone number on it. "She's a retired cop. Good as they come. Reasonable rates. You'll like her."

"Thanks." Tyler took the card. "Can I buy you lunch now? It's early, but I'm hungry."

"A good county sheriff never turns down a free meal." Wayne stood up. "The Longhorn?"

"Is there any other place?"

"Dottie'd shoot us both if she found out we were sneaking around to other restaurants."

"You've got that right." Laughing, they left the room and headed outside. The day had turned warm, and Tyler slung his jacket over his shoulder. The two men enjoyed the short walk to the Longhorn.

But as they reached the coffee shop, Wayne Jackson made a mental connection. "You know, being at the Longhorn reminds me," Wayne said. "There was this guy this morning who came in, asking something. Directions or something. Anyway, some of us were talking about Lynn and that horse of hers."

Tyler stopped.

"And the guy acted real interested. In fact, he was listening in on our talk, as far as I could tell. Bothered me, but I didn't think much of it, then. Looked like a city boy, too. And when he left, he seemed right shook up. Like maybe something he'd heard had bothered him."

"Did he have two little girls with him? Drive a red Subaru?"

"He did."

"That's our man. Sam Russell has two little kids. He brought them out to the ranch just this morning to look around and visit."

"Well, it had to be just a coincidence. Us talking about her when he came in and all. No way that could have been planned."

"No."

"No way at all."

"SO WHAT DO YOU THINK NOW?" Lynn leaned against the wall by Lightning and waited for Sam's response to the documents and photographs she had just shown him.

"You have a lot of faith in yourself," he said finally. His expression was thoughtful, somber.

That was not the kind of reply she'd expected. "I suppose I do," she admitted. "But if you don't, you shouldn't be in an occupation that depends on self-confidence."

"In horse as well as rider, if I understand what you've said."

"That's right."

Sam thought for a moment. "Lynn, what happens to your dreams if something happens to Lightning?"

"It won't!" She sat up straighter. "I'll see to that!"

"But what if..." He paused. "How old are you?"

"What's that got to do with anything?"

"Twenty? Twenty-two?"

"I'm twenty-five."

"I see." He got up and walked toward the colt's stall. Lightning's big black eyes watched him carefully. "Lynn, I'm thirty-five. When I was your age, I didn't think anything could happen to my dreams, either. Things were almost perfect. Then, it ended. My wife died suddenly. The worst thing that could happen, did."

She had nothing to say to that.

"It did, and now I'm rebuilding. But I tell you, it isn't easy. Some days, it seems impossible." He turned, and she saw pain in his face.

"Sam, I—"

"I see in you such hope and trust in fate. But, Lynn, I have to tell you I have no such faith. I don't believe in happy endings. You take whatever you can get. That's about it. About all any of us can hope for."

"Oh, Sam."

He turned around. "Hey, don't be feeling sorry for me. I just want you to be aware that no one's immune to pain."

"I know that! I lost my mother six years ago. Just when she and I were becoming real friends, in addition to the mother and daughter we'd always been. Don't tell me about loss. I know." She stood up, her hands curling into fists at her side.

"But you don't act like it." He backed up as she stepped forward. "You act like a kid who thinks Christmas Day guarantees presents. You seem to think that if the three of us will just go along with your ideas, everything will work out, and this nag of yours will win the damn Triple Crown at a walk!"

"That is not what I said, Sam Russell." She took another step toward him, and he stepped back. "All I said was that I want a decent chance. I want to be trusted to do what I do best—to understand and run this horse."

Sam nodded, but he took another step away from her.

And Lightning, who was directly behind him, butted him a good shove with his nose and sent him stumbling forward.

Right into Lynn's arms.

The impact took her breath away, and for a moment, she stood in his embrace, her lips parted, her eyes gazing up at him.

And Sam kissed her.

And Lynn kissed him back.

Until an unpleasant thought occurred to her.

He might think she was doing this to influence him, to persuade him to help her in her plans for Lightning!

Lynn pushed away from him. "I—I...I'm sorry," she stammered. "I don't know what...um, made me do that. I don't usually...I mean, I just don't know why..."

"I do." He touched her face, but didn't try to reinstate the embrace. His smile was warm, his expression a little stunned. As if the moment had shaken him up as much as it had her. "Lightning over there butted me right into your arms. You and your horse have this scheme to seduce my mind and my body so that I'll go along with you both and—"

"Oh, don't flatter yourself!" She regretted the words immediately. "Oh, I didn't...I'm sorry. I mean..." She crossed her arms protectively. "Oh, damn."

"I was kidding, Lynn." He moved slowly toward her. "Come on. I don't believe you're a schemer, and I know the horse can't be, either."

Lightning chose that moment to let out a shrill whinny. He stomped around in his stall as if he would deny that insult. Sam and Lynn turned to look at him, then at each other.

Then they started to laugh. They moved together and put their arms around each other and laughed.

And then they kissed again. Slowly, gently, carefully, experimentally.

"Oh," Lynn said softly after a while. "Oh, my."

"Yeah," Sam agreed. "My, my."

"Um." Lynn stepped back from him again. "This...this is kind of..." She pushed her hair back nervously.

"Unexpected," he finished. He rubbed the back of his neck. "At least to me. Lynn, I swear I had no intention of—"

"I believe you." She went back over to the horse. "And as for me, you ought to know by now that there's only one guy in my life these days. And he's only two years old and has four legs. So..."

J.T. HAD HAD enough. For the past thirty minutes he had been listening to the little girls and Lettie Mae giggling in the kitchen. It wasn't that he disliked children—on the contrary, he had actually enjoyed the sound of their laughter. But as time passed and there was no sign of their father or Lynn, J.T. decided it was time to take things in hand.

"There you are!" he said as he strode into the stable. "I saw the children in the kitchen. Wondered where their papa had gotten to."

"Hi, Daddy. This is Sam Russell. Sam, my father, J.T. McKinney."

The two men shook hands and J.T. seemed about to say something when another voice floated toward them.

"Well, now. Here's that horsie you came to see, gals." Hank Travis's lean form limped slowly into the stable. Two little girls were on his left and right.

Sandy looked at Lynn. Then she spotted Lightning, who had his head and neck stretched out of the stall, watching the humans with obvious, deep curiosity. "That's him?" She walked right up to the horse and patted his nose.

"Sandy, don't!" Sam reached for his daughter and lifted her away from the horse. "He doesn't know you. He might bite." Deprived of attention, Lightning snorted, bared his teeth again and squealed in anger. His hind hooves hit the side of the stall, and the stable shook.

"Daddy." Allie stepped up to the stall. "He's not mean. Mrs. Reese said so." She demonstrated by touching the quivering nose. Lynn was right at her side immediately, monitoring Lightning's reaction. But Lightning, happy to be touched again, relaxed and let himself be petted.

"Um, Allie," Lynn said. "He's not mean, but he is startled and upset. I don't think you understand how a horse thinks."

"Oh, yes, she does," Sandy declared, pushing away from her father's grasp. "He's thinking he needs to do something to let everybody know he's worth what you say he is." She looked at Hank. "Mr. Travis doesn't like him."

Hank grinned. "He's a worthless hunk of dog food. Ought to sell him for scraps. Ugly critter."

"That's mean!"

"He is not ugly! He's beautiful!"

Both girls chorused defense of Lightning. Hank's grin widened. He was clearly having a ball, teasing them.

Lynn turned to the girls. "Want to meet Lightning? Really meet him?" she asked. "Your daddy does own part of him, you know."

"Which part? Front or back?" Sandy giggled. Allie hit her arm, but she was grinning, too.

"Daddy, why don't you and Grandpa take Sam up to the house and offer him some coffee or something? We girls have things to do."

Hank regarded Sam. "You like your bourbon with or without branch water?" he asked. "Or do you drink that sissy stuff my great-grandson's planning to make. Wine?"

Sam hesitated. "I don't drink much ordinarily, but I do like a good sippin' bourbon." He looked at Hank. "Learned to appreciate it from my own grandpappy. He was a Louisiana man."

"Huh. Not much good, then." Hank glared back, waiting for a retort.

"Come on, Sam." J.T. covered a smile. "Let's go up to the house." He took his grandfather's arm. "You too, Grandpa. It's near your nap time, isn't it?"

"Nope. Ain't had lunch yet. Besides, the one little missy with the big mouth said she'd play cards with me later on. Said she'd whup me, too." He chuckled. "As if a little girl could beat me at poker."

"Just don't make any bets you can't cover, Grandpa," Lynn warned him. "Or any promises you might regret."

Hank was still laughing as the men made their way to the house.

"Miss McKinney, can we really pet him when we want?" Allie interrupted Lynn's musing. "I mean, will he bite, like Daddy said?"

"Thoroughbred horses are different from other animals," Lynn explained. "They're kind of jumpy and edgy all the time because all they want to do is get out of their stalls and run. So..."

"So, why don't you let him?" Sandy was looking at the horse, pity in her eyes. "If that's what he wants and if you really love him?"

"It's because I really love him that I won't," Lynn said. "Not yet, anyway." She reached up and scratched her horse behind his ears. He made a contented, rumbling noise. "He could run now, but then he wouldn't be able to run the big races later. And that's what he really wants to do, even though he doesn't know it yet."

"How come?"

Lynn thought. "What do you like to do most?"

The girls shrugged. "Play..." they said in unison.

"Cards," Allie said.

"Music," Sandy said.

"But when you were very little, did you know that?"

A cloud seemed to fall over both children. "I don't remember being little," Sandy said.

"I do. Some," Allie said. She looked upset.

Lynn kicked herself. "Okay. Wrong question. Let me try again. Suppose you knew that in the future, someday, you'd... um... be rich and famous. But in order to get there, you had to do some really hard work that you didn't always like."

The girls watched her, but said nothing.

"Okay. Another shot. Let's just talk about Lightning here. He's two years old. He's—"

"He's just a baby!" Sandy's eyes were wide. "And he's so big!"

"He sure is." Lynn gathered the girls to her sides, and opened the stall, leaving just the leather gate strap in place to keep Lightning inside. The horse whickered a welcome.

"When he's four or five," Lynn said, as the girls became acquainted with the animal, "he'll get to quit racing and go be... um, whatever he wants to be." She didn't think this was the time to explain what a stud was and what he did for a living. "But now, I am his teacher and even if it seems hard, he has to do what I know is the best for him so he can be the greatest racehorse ever!"

"You like to ride him when he's racing?" Allie asked.

Lynn felt a glow. "I sure do. I love it! There's no other thing like it in the world. He feels like part of me when we run. And when we race, I feel like we can outrun the wind!"

"Wow," said Sandy.

"Could we ever ride him?" Allie asked.

"Not yet. He's too young to be ridden for pleasure. He's still in training for racing. When he retires, maybe he would let you get on him and just walk around." Lynn stroked Lightning's nose. "But someday you might learn to ride like I do, and perhaps you can ride one of his sons or daughters in a race."

Both girls looked at her. She read puzzlement, excitement and perhaps a little awe in their expressions. Then their attention went back to Lightning as he pushed forward, whickering, as if he wanted to be the center of the universe once more.

"He tickles." Sandy giggled as Lightning nibbled at her hair. "He likes me."

"Sure he does," Lynn said. "You're being nice to him. As long as he's treated well, he's a sweetie."

"Then don't ever hurt him," Allie advised. She was old enough to still be cautious, even though she was caressing Lightning as happily as her little sister.

"I won't," Lynn declared. *All I need do,* she added silently, *is to convince your daddy that my way is the best way.*

"YOU KNOW, Tyler, your little sister may not be as far off the mark as all of us thought. Thoroughbred racing's starting to get popular down here in quarter horse country. Since pari-mutuel betting's been legal, the racetracks are starting to get serious about it. Dedicated race fans find quarter horses just don't run a long enough or exciting enough race. When I was out in Nevada, I saw the kind of profits that can come in if the public supports a sport. Little Lynn may just be a bit ahead of the times."

Tyler dismissed the sheriff's comments with a wave of his hand. "I know there're a few tracks that're set up for longer races, but seems Texas is as prejudiced against her kind of horse as it is against my kind of drink."

"Wine versus bourbon." Wayne grinned. "No contest. Not yet."

"Not yet. But there's always the future. Anyway, Lynn's more interested in the big, national races for Lightning. What she's fighting against is the intention of her other investors to limit him to local runs."

"If they have money problems, I can see why they'd want to keep the horse out of the big time. It costs, you know. Big, big bucks."

"I guess I really hadn't paid any attention. I didn't realize..."

"Tyler, guys invest millions in the right horse. And make millions from it. *If* things go well."

"There's that little word again. If... How many times a day do Ruth or I say it? If the weather's right, if the rainfall's sufficient, but not too much, if the sun doesn't get too hot, if...if...if..." He laughed. "Lynn and I. Seems like we both took on dreams that are if-dependent."

The sheriff didn't join in the laughter. "Yeah, but if she was my little sister, I'd want to know more about the guys in business with her, and I'd take a real close look at their financial records."

"Okay, then." Tyler got up and slid a five-dollar tip under his coffee saucer. "It's time to visit this private eye."

CHAPTER SIX

FATE PREVENTED Sam Russell from accepting Cynthia's invitation to stay for lunch. Just as they had all settled down in the comfortable den and were enjoying a pre-meal glass of Rebel Yell sour mash Kentucky bourbon, Sam's beeper went off.

"My answering service," he explained, shutting off the annoying sound. "They know not to page me when I'm this far out of town, unless it's an emergency. I hate to do this, but mind if I use your phone?"

"Of course not. Use the phone in the office."

A minute later, Sam returned to the den. "I have to leave immediately. One of my patients has been in an automobile accident. There's been some facial injury involving his teeth and the doctor wants to consult with me. I apologize for rushing off. Please explain to the kids and tell them I'll be back to fetch them."

Sam's mind was on his patient, and on Lynn McKinney, when he hit the highway leading out of

Crystal Creek toward Austin, and he didn't notice the speedometer needle rising.

It also took him a few seconds to notice the reflection of blue and red bar lights in his rearview mirror.

Wayne Jackson had been doing a postlunch cruise of the road just outside of town, thinking about his conversation with Tyler, when the red Subaru had come sailing by, clocking nearly eighty. Wayne had considered the situation, smiled to himself and hit the lights.

No point in using the siren unless the guy tried to ignore him or run.

He didn't. Pulled on over to the shoulder, stayed in the car but rolled down his window and sat still as a stone, while Wayne made a call in to the dispatcher and then got out, ticket clipboard in hand. Wayne was satisfied the guy was going to behave. But before he walked over to the red car, he slipped on his mirrored sunglasses and smiled to himself again. This was likely to be some fun. Time to see what this dentist fellow was made up of. He could report his findings to Tyler, if he learned anything interesting.

After noticing the guy eavesdropping and after talking to Tyler, he was pretty sure he didn't like this old Austin boy much. Not much at all. Wayne wiped any expression from his face and cleared his throat, aiming for deep bass intimidation. He didn't do this kind of thing very often, but when it was called for, he knew how. Surely did know how.

Sam sat, waiting. He was guilty. No question about it. But, dammit, he needed to get to the hospital. People were waiting for him. He tapped his fingertips on the wheel.

"Afternoon, sir." The cop was at the window, looking in. Mirrored glasses reflected Sam's face back at him. "You in some kind of hurry?" His tone was dry, almost mocking.

"As a matter of fact, I am, Officer." Sam handed out his driver's license and professional identification card. "You see, I'm a dentist. I just got an emergency call from—"

"Sir, have you been drinking?" The cop leaned in a little farther and sniffed. He frowned. "I do believe I smell liquor."

Sam froze. Then he got defensive. "No. That is... I had a sip, but—"

"Mind getting out of the car, sir?" The cop stepped back, motioning with a big hand. "Now, please."

Angry and frustrated, Sam complied. Then he remembered seeing this officer somewhere. "Don't I know you?" he asked, looking more closely at the man.

"No, sir." The cop stared at him from behind the mirrors. "Now, please do exactly what I tell you. Place one hand..."

So Sam went through the routine of driver-sobriety testing with his temper edging toward a precipice and his mind telling him to hang on for dear life. He *had* been speeding, and he *did* smell like bourbon, thanks to the sip or two he'd had back at the ranch, but...

Then it hit him where he'd seen the policeman. "I know," he said, stopping in midstride while doing the line-walk. "I saw you in that little café back in Crystal Creek. You were with those other guys who were talking about Lynn McKinney."

The cop just stared some more. "Finish walking the line, please, sir."

"Listen." Sam stopped and turned around. "Just call J.T. McKinney, will you? He'll tell you I didn't drink—"

"Sir, I advise you to finish walking that line."

"I'm a dentist, dammit! They're waiting surgery for me at the hospital. Call J.T.!"

"Sir, are you refusing to walk that line?"

Sam hesitated, so close to the edge he could smell his own frustrated anger. And then he saw the corner of the cop's mouth twitch. It hit him. The son of a bitch was *enjoying* this.

For a man with Scottish, Irish and Creole ancestors, that was just too much to endure. A man had his pride, after all.

So, Sam Russell lost it.

"WOULD YOU GIRLS LIKE some more dessert?" Cynthia asked the Russell children hopefully. It was fun having kids at the table. And these youngsters ate as if they wouldn't be getting another decent meal for months! "There's plenty."

"Well . . ." Allie and Sandy glanced at each other.

"It's sure good," Sandy said. "I'd like more, please."

"You, too, honey?" Cynthia asked Allie.

"Yes, ma'am. If it's not too much trouble." Allie went after her second helping with enthusiasm.

After she was finished, Hank said, "Say, scamp, you still wanna play cards with me after lunch?"

"Sure, Mr. Travis." Allie's smile was innocent, her eyes guileless. "Penny a point?"

"Be very careful, Grandpa," Lynn said, her attention directed at her dessert, her smile hidden. "And don't go squalling later I didn't warn you."

Hank just chuckled some more.

"J.T." Virginia Parks appeared in the dining room doorway. The housekeeper had begged off lunch, saying she was trying to lose a few pounds before springtime. "Phone call for you."

"Who is it, Virginia? I'd rather call back after we're done here."

"It's Wayne Jackson." Virginia bent over and whispered in her boss's ear.

"He what!" J.T. exploded from the chair and left the dining room in a rush.

"Virginia?" Cynthia started to get up. "What's wrong?"

"Not anything for you to worry about," Virginia assured her. "I just thought it was something J.T. needed to straighten out right away," she added.

"Must be about Cal," Hank declared. "Boy's always out getting hisself into hot water."

"No, it's not Cal," Virginia replied. "It's not about the family this time."

Lynn felt a slight tinge of alarm. "Virginia, when did Sam Russell leave here?"

"I'm not sure, honey." Virginia didn't look at Lynn directly. "He had some kind of hospital emergency, I believe."

"Daddy doesn't go to the hospital very much." Sandy stirred the mushy remains of her dessert. "Not like Mama did."

"Your mama a sawbones?" Hank asked, his tone gentle for a change.

"Huh?" Sandy frowned up at him. "What's that?"

"It means a doctor," her older sister explained. "She's dead," she added.

"So's Lynn's mama," Hank said. "But now she's got Missy Boston here to be her stepmama. So, she's got someone to talk to that ain't a man, anyways."

Allie looked at Hank. "I like talking to men. They listen to me."

"How old you say you are, young'n?"

"Eleven. Going on twelve."

"Lord God." Hank stood up. "They're startin' Charm School early these days. Come on, kiddo. Let's play some cards."

"Okay." Allie got up and followed the old man out of the dining room.

Lynn turned to Sandy. "Want to see our music room?" she asked.

"A music room?" The child's eyes widened. "You have one like Professor Bailey?"

Lynn laughed. "Not exactly. It's part of the attic. When we were little, Daddy used to holler so about the awful noises we made playing the piano and stuff that my mother had all the instruments moved way up to the corner of the attic, so he couldn't hear us."

Sandy laughed at that. "You must all be pretty bad."

"Well, we're sure not like you. But once my brothers and I thought we could make a country and western band all by ourselves. We had fun, anyway."

Sandy was quiet for a time. "I wish we had a real family like you do."

Lynn wanted to tell the child that she did have a great family with her sister and her father, but something held the words back.

Sandy stared off into space. "It's nice with all these people," she said. "It's nice. I wish... I like it."

"Well," Lynn said, "you're welcome to come here and hang out with us anytime, Sandy. Come on. Let's go upstairs."

Sandy lost her melancholy expression and pushed her chair back. "I gotta carry my plate into the kitchen first," she said. "Then I can do what I want." She grinned at Lynn. "Those're Daddy's rules. I guess Allie forgot."

"I'll take hers," Lynn said.

They both carried their dessert plates into the kitchen. Then Lynn showed Sandy the back stairs leading from the kitchen up to the second floor.

"It's kind of spooky," Sandy said as they made their way up the final set of stairs—a pull-down ladder that creaked dramatically underfoot. "Like a haunted house."

"No ghosts," Lynn said. "I guarantee it. We drove 'em all out years ago with the racket we made up here."

Sandy turned around. "Maybe they came back because it's been too quiet."

"Shhh, then. We'll surprise them."

Sandy giggled and continued up the ladder. Lynn followed right behind her and reached up to turn on the lights.

"Oh," said Sandy.

"Yeah," Lynn responded. "Neat, isn't it?"

A lump formed in her throat.

She hadn't been up here since before her mother died. She'd still been in college, actually, and had needed some old family letters for a paper she was writing. The trunk over in the corner that she'd rummaged through to find the letters was still open.

"The music stuff's way down there," she said, pointing to the other end of the long attic. "Over our bedrooms, so we wouldn't disturb Mama or Daddy so much if we played at night."

"You could come up here whenever you wanted, couldn't you? And you could do stuff and play and not bother anybody. Not get yelled at for keeping anyone awake."

Lynn thought about that. "You have a problem at home with when you can practice?"

Sandy shook her head. "Not about practice. Professor Bailey insists on three hours a day, and I do it. I'm talking about just playing." She sighed and wandered over to the open trunk. "Sometimes, in the middle of the night, I hear... I hear this music in my head and want like crazy to go play it. But I can't, 'cause our house is too small and if I did, it'd wake up Daddy and Allie.''

"What about that music school in Chicago? Would they let you play anytime?"

Sandy nodded.

Lynn hesitated. To comment on the obvious solution to Sandy's problem might place Lynn in the middle of an emotional mine field. This probably had to be handled very carefully. Poor Sam! No wonder he'd been desperate enough to ask for her help. He wasn't asking for much—just for her to be friends with his girls.

And thank goodness that's all she was in for! She really had no business trying to help this child. She had almost no experience with kids. She certainly didn't want to make things worse.

But that didn't mean she and the girls couldn't have a good time today.

HOURS LATER, Sam Russell drove back along the route he'd traced that morning. He slowed, making sure he was at least ten miles below the speed limit. If it hadn't been for J.T.'s intervention, he'd likely still be cooling his heels in jail in Crystal Creek!

But that was all over and done with, and Sam had vowed to keep the incident quiet. He had been driving too fast. He had smelled like liquor, and he had lost his temper. In a way, he'd asked for the trouble he got, and once the air was cleared, why, that Jackson guy had provided a police escort for him right up to the front entrance of the hospital, so the treatment of his injured patient had not been delayed.

Twilight was settling on the land when he drove through the front gates of the Double C. The sky was painted with the last streaks of the spectacular sunset, the air was clear as glass—no city pollution here—and the ground was beginning to come to life with green shoots cover and a spot or two of color from wildflowers.

He drove on toward the ranch, thinking about Lynn. Her kiss had been a surprise. A pleasant one. Sam took the turn into the ranch house drive at a little more speed than he should have and gravel flew. He slowed and stopped in front. Immediately, the big door opened and J.T. came down the steps to greet him.

"Sam," he said. "I'm sorry as I can be about what happened. Wayne just took it in his head you'd had too much to drink when he smelled you *had* been drinking that bourbon. I guess he overreacted. He's a good cop, believe me."

Sam got out of the car. "I understand. Listen, it was my fault, and I appreciate your coming to my rescue. If I hadn't been such a hothead, losing my temper like I did, Jackson never would have taken me in. And he did rush me into the city with his siren and lights, so I was there in time for the surgery.''

"I'm glad it worked out, then." J.T. gave him a friendly slap on the back. "Come on inside. You have to stay for dinner."

"Oh, I don't—"

"Come on. Your kids are terrific. They've kept busy and happy all afternoon." J.T. laughed. "Your oldest skunked my grandpa at cards and—"

"Daddy!" Sandy came running down the steps. "You have to see this place up in the attic! Lynn's got..." She threw herself at her father.

Sam caught her up in his arms, amazed at the animation in her face and voice. "Lynn's got what? And isn't it *Miss* McKinney?"

"Not after the jam session we just had. We're definitely on a first-name basis now." Lynn appeared in the doorway. Her slender body was silhouetted by the light from the house, and he couldn't see her face clearly. But his heart suddenly took off at breakneck speed.

"We ought to be on Bourbon Street," she added, laughing and moving down the steps toward them.

"Bourbon Street?" Sam looked away from the woman to the girl. "What's that mean? You played jazz?"

"Sure did." Sandy wriggled out of his embrace. "And Lynn's hot, let me tell you!"

"I think I—"

"Daddy!" Allie came out the door. "I just finished winning a hundred dollars from Hank! He paid me in old gold coins, too!" She held up her hand. Gold winked and caught the last red rays of the setting sun.

Sam tried to catch up. "I thought you hated jazz, Sandy," he said. "And, Allie, you can't keep that money. It's too valuable."

"Daddy!" Allie's voice rose. "I won them. He bet them. So they're mine!"

"No, young lady, I—"

"Cool down, boy." Hank Travis limped out onto the front porch and took a seat in the rocking chair. "The girl whipped me, fair and square. Ain't seen a player like her in all my born days, I'll be happy to tell you."

"But, Mr. Travis. Sir... *Gold* coins?"

"They *were* his," J.T. said, giving Sam another friendly slap on the back. "And no one has ever been able to tell my grandpappy what to do with what's his."

Sam swallowed hard against his rising concern. Allie's tone had been too whiny and defiant. She was using these people and their good nature to get around his rules, and they both knew it.

But they were guests right now, and to make an issue of it would be to violate good manners.

"Sam." Lynn laid a hand on his arm. "Did Daddy ask you to stay for dinner?" she asked. "I . . . we really wish you would." Her smile was hesitant, almost apologetic, as if she knew what kind of turmoil Allie's behavior was causing him.

"Thank you," he said. "It's kind of you. I didn't have any plans for—" Sandy moved into the light coming through the front door. "What have you been in?" Sam exclaimed. "You've got cobwebs in your hair!" Actually, the cobwebs in her hair were the least of it. The child was filthy, her face smudged with what looked like soot and her clothing dusty and even torn in places.

"We were playing up in the attic," Sandy replied. "That's where the music stuff is. It's great. Lynn can go up there and make noise anytime she wants and not bother anyone. I wish we had—"

"It's just a soundproofed playroom in a corner of the house," Lynn said, putting her hands on Sandy's shoulders. "My brothers and I had some old instruments up there, so I thought Sandy'd get a kick out of seeing them." She brushed at the child's shirt with her hand, to little effect. "I guess we got into some of the old trunks, too. Looking for sheet music and costumes. That's where the dust and dirt came from." She shrugged, and he saw that she was even dustier and more cobwebbed than Sandy.

"It was great." Sandy's smile was wide. "We had fun and got dirty," she added, as if one were the necessary ingredient for the other.

"Sorry," said Lynn. A smudge of soot ran along one fine cheekbone, giving her a childlike, vulnerable look.

Sam melted. He was being foolish, making a fuss about any of this, he decided. "I shouldn't have snapped." He put his hand on his daughter's head. "I know I'm a bit of a cleanliness freak." He reached for Sandy's hand. "Comes from my profession, I suppose."

Hank spoke up. "When I was a young'n, the only dentist in the territory was a butcher who'd yank a good tooth 'longside of a bad one just to hear you yell twice." Hank chuckled. "Think he liked it."

"We've come far in dentistry, Mr. Travis," Sam replied. "Nowadays, with all the resources available, no one has to feel pain at the dentist's hands. We leave that up to folks with real bad attitudes and sharp tongues."

Hank's grin glowed out of his tanned, wrinkled face. "Point made, boy. You stay for dinner. You're all right. You and your brats."

Lynn held out her hand. "Come on, Sandy. I'll show you where you can wash up. I think we might even have some clean clothes over in the guest house that might just fit you.''

''Guest house?'' Allie stepped forward. ''You have a guest house?''

Lynn pointed. ''It's that place over there across the yard. When we were little, the main house was just too noisy and full of action for most company to tolerate, so...''

''So I had some extra rooms built and put them under a separate roof,'' J.T. finished. ''Made for a happier visit for one. In fact, it's being occupied right now by Ruth, although I believe she and Tyler have gone into town.''

''Show us.'' Sandy turned to Lynn and took her hand.

''I've never been in a guest house,'' Allie declared, taking the other hand.

''It's right this way,'' Lynn said, leading them toward the lawn between the driveway and the outer buildings. ''Come with me.''

And Sam watched the three of them move away from him into the twilight.

LYNN FELT him watching her all through dinner. Before the meal, she had escorted both girls to the guest house, seen to it that Sandy was scrubbed squeaky-clean and that both she and Allie were brushed and combed and presentable. Lynn had made a game out of it, and they'd had fun. Almost as if the three of them were sisters.

Since the guest house was used for storage as well as for company, she had been able to find clean clothes, too. It helped that, though an adult, she was not much bigger than the girls, so her more recent rejects were at least slightly stylish. She'd allowed them to pick and choose outfits from the selection available. Much giggling and teasing had been involved in the process, but they'd emerged looking relatively civilized. Even their father had seemed to appreciate her efforts with his offspring. He'd thanked her, and his eyes had spoken more than a simple thanks.

So, why was Sam Russell looking so pensive? she wondered. Almost unhappy. He hardly said two consecutive words during the meal, although he behaved politely and acted as if he was enjoying himself. But he was content to let the conversation roll around him like surf on a beach, rather than plunging directly into the water himself.

Even his girls noticed. "Daddy, are you all right?" Allie asked after a while. "Did anything bad happen at the hospital?"

"No, honey." Sam smiled at her. His gaze wavered to Allie and then back to Lynn. "Everything at the hospital went well. The man who had his teeth damaged is fine now. We fixed him right up in no time. And I'm fine."

"Sure?"

"Just fine."

"More sweet potatoes?" Lettie Mae was doing thirds. Everyone, including Silent Sam, had eaten heartily and the cook was beaming with delight. This was her kind of dinner.

When the feast was finally over, Sandy made an announcement. "Um, Lynn and I made up a song today. Would anybody like to hear it?"

"No!" Lynn declared. "They wouldn't!"

"Oh, yeah!" Allie beat her hand on the table. "Come on. Do it!"

"I wanna hear it," Hank declared, playing along. He reached into his pocket and pulled out another gleaming gold coin. "This'n's yours, littlest Russell girl, if you can get Lynnie to sing for us."

"No fair," Lynn said.

"Oh, come on." Sandy stood up and grabbed her hand. "We're good. You know it. Let's do it!"

Lynn glanced at Sam. His eyes were unreadable, but he was smiling. An almost quizzical smile, as if he was not sure how to react. Her father, Cynthia, Virginia and Lettie Mae also began to coax Lynn.

"Okay, okay," Lynn said. "I know when I'm outnumbered. Let's do it."

A LITTLE before ten o'clock in the driveway in front of the Double C ranch house, Tyler and Ruth got out of their pickup. Cal and Serena unloaded right behind them from Cal's truck. "Think having all of us home for a Saturday night will give Daddy heart failure?" Cal joked as they went up the steps, arms around one another. "The four of us at once?"

"He's liable to move out to the guest house himself tonight," Tyler said. He wasn't really in the mood for a big family get-together after his talk with Wayne Jackson that morning, but Cal and Serena had driven in from Wolverton and the two couples had met in the drugstore at Crystal Creek. One thing had led to another, and here they all were.

Or rather, here they were after having shared more than one pitcher of beer out at Zack's. He, of course, was quite sober. He couldn't speak for the other three. "Try not to get too rowdy," he added. "Daddy's been kind of...well, touchy lately."

Cal kissed Serena. "Okay," he said. "Serena and me'll just go straight up to bed and..."

"Cal, hush." Serena giggled. "I'm staying with Ruthie in the guest house, and you know that. Can you just imagine what Hank would have to say if I spent the night in your room?"

"Awww," said Cal, clutching at his chest. "My heart's just broke!" He stopped. Listened. "Hey, what's that? They killing a cat in there?"

"Sounds like music." Tyler walked to the door.

"Not any music I ever heard in this house," Cal declared, pushing his hat back on his head and opening the door. "Hey!" he yelled. "Anybody home?"

A blast of noise answered him.

"They ain't killing a cat," Cal declared, looking at the other three. "They're being killed by a mountain lion!"

"Come on." Tyler was laughing. "Sounds like it's out in the sun room. Let's go see."

They made their way through the dining room and stopped in the doorway to the sunroom. They could hardly believe what they saw. Eight people ceased what they were doing and looked up at them.

Each person held a musical instrument of some sort. Hank had a mouth harp, Lynn a tambourine, and a little girl next to her had a battered violin tucked under her small chin. Tyler recognized the instrument as the one his mother had made him take lessons on. How many years ago...? Lettie Mae held a washboard. Even J.T. gripped a pair of maracas. He smiled. "Evening, boys, Ruth, Serena. Want to join in? Grab something to play."

"Uh," Cal said, stunned. "Hi, Daddy. What's going on?"

"It's a jam session," Lynn explained. She was sitting next to a good-looking blond guy Cal didn't recognize. "Go get your guitar, Cal. Tyler, can you still play the harmonica?"

"Uh," Cal repeated. Tyler said nothing. The women were laughing.

"Who are they?" one of the children asked Lynn. "Are they your brothers?"

Lynn made the introductions. Cal came to and gave a whoop. "You're the dentist!" he declared, shaking hands with Sam Russell. "Hey, glad to meet you, man." He turned to the children. "These your girls, Sam? Hey, darlin's. I'm Cal."

Hank started twanging on the harp. Cal grabbed Serena around the waist and they danced. She reached out a hand and pulled Allie into the jig, and Tyler took Sandy, along with Ruth.

Sam sat back in his chair, watching the Mc-Kinneys and his children. *Dear Lord,* he thought. *How could I give them this? This is what they need. Family. Lots of loving, fun family. Not just me and a hired lady to watch them after school.*

He looked at Lynn.

She held out her hand. "Care to dance?"

Sam smiled. "I have two left feet," he warned.

"It won't matter in here. There's no room to get fancy or critical. Come on!"

As they danced, Sam became increasingly aware of Lynn as a desirable woman. Her body was small and hard with muscle, but rounded in all the right places.

And she moved like a dream with a natural athletic grace and skill. Her auburn hair came out of its restrictive ponytail and bounced around her laughing face as she danced with him. Her eyes shone with life and joy. And ...

And Sam found himself enchanted beyond expectation.

Then, when everyone was panting and laughing from the fun and exertion of dancing, Hank set down his mouth harp and said, "Okay, little Russell. Play us some fiddle music. And make it good old-fashioned stuff," he added, winking.

Allie whispered something to her little sister, and they both giggled.

"Are you sure I should?" Sandy asked Allie.

Allie nodded. More giggles followed.

Sandy didn't miss a beat. She left Tyler and Ruth, picked up the old violin, made some adjustments to the strings and started in.

Sam listened in astonishment as his daughter played country and western music he wasn't even aware she'd ever heard. Hank applauded and yipped like a coyote. The rest clapped along, adding an occasional yell or war whoop as the music dictated.

Around midnight, the party broke up. After declining Cynthia and J.T.'s invitation to spend the night at the ranch, Sam and Lynn tucked the very sleepy children in the back seat of the Subaru, wrap-

ping them in blankets borrowed from the Mc-
Kinneys. The moon was low in the sky, and the stars
were bright, filling the dark bowl of heaven. It was a
sight Sam didn't often see in the city.

Sam turned to Lynn. His real feelings were too
deep and confused for him to express, so he offered
only a polite thanks. "It's really nice of you people
to take my kids in like you have today. I don't think
they've ever experienced anything quite like this day
and evening."

Lynn smiled. "I don't know that my family has,
either. Sandy's violin playing really impressed them."

Sam dismissed that with a wave of his hand. "You
should hear her play classical. She wasn't playing
seriously tonight. Just having fun."

"So were the rest of us."

"No kidding!" he teased, his mood lightening
again. "For a while there, it was difficult to tell who
were the grown-ups and who were the kids. I haven't
danced and joked and played like that in a long, long
time." He grew more serious, trying to put his emotions into words, to express what he had realized this
evening. He glanced at his children in the car, then
back at Lynn. "You have a wonderful family, Lynn.
Do you know how lucky you are?"

"I think so." She stood still, her arms folded.

"I don't think my kids have ever really felt that
kind of security."

"Sam, I believe you're wrong about that. They love you, and you love them."

"Of course. Maybe I... But I don't think I've done enough."

"Then do something about it."

"Don't you think I would if I knew how? What do you think drove me to ask you, a stranger, to help me?"

"I don't know, Sam. What did?"

He resisted her allure for a moment. But the starlight on her face made her look soft as a magnolia petal, and her dark eyes were challenging him. "I think," he said, touching her cheek, "that maybe this was part of it." He bent his head and kissed her again. As their lips touched, he drew her close in a gentle embrace.

Lynn felt herself respond to him as she had the first time. It was a warmth that began deep inside. Unsettling but pleasant. She wanted more.

But he stopped the kiss almost immediately, broke the embrace and stepped away from her. He put his hands in his pockets. "Sorry," he said. "I guess I can't blame the horse this time."

"Why try to place blame at all?"

He shrugged, but didn't answer.

Seeing his discomfort, Lynn didn't wait for his answer. "The girls had a great time. You should bring them out again soon," she said.

"Thanks. And if you have no objections, I'd still like you to keep on seeing them."

She laughed. "Of course I have no objections! I had a terrific time with them today. But, Sam..."

"What?"

"I like you. I really like your kids. But I..."

He waited, giving her time.

"I don't want any of that to influence you about Lightning. I want any decision you make about the racing to be free and clear of any...uh..."

"Emotional entanglements?"

"Yes."

His relief was evident. "That puts into words just what I was struggling to say. I like you, too." He framed her face with his hands. "But I'll keep my feelings out of any decisions about the horse. I really did listen to what you had to say this morning, and I think your arguments are sound. I'll take it up with Phil and Dan right away. I can't make promises, but I'll get them to at least listen. Then we can all sit down and discuss it."

"If you can just do that, I know I can get them into my camp!"

"You really are the confident one, aren't you?" He kissed her forehead. "But I guess that's what it takes to make a potential winner."

"That's right. It's a matter of attitude as much as anything else. Hard work and a winning attitude!"

"So you tell me." He smiled at her. "So can we set up some time next week for you and the girls to spend together?"

"Anytime. Except for the hours I work Lightning early in the mornings, I'm free."

"My life is more scheduled, so if you have a chance to get into the city, just give my housekeeper a call and plan to come by. I'll tell her about you and the girls on Monday."

"Okay."

"As for the personal part of our relationship, I'll be in touch with you," he said. "Soon."

Then he got into his car and was gone.

CHAPTER SEVEN

ALL DAY SUNDAY, Lynn moved in a sort of daze, trying to make sense of what had happened the day and night before. Sam's kisses lingered in her memory, a tantalizing promise of what might happen between them ... once the business with Lightning was resolved.

Meanwhile she endured a fair amount of good-natured teasing from her family about her guests, particularly about handsome Sam. But it was tempered by the fact that they had all enjoyed the three Russells nearly as much as she had. Sam's calm, polite manner had impressed everyone, especially since he'd had good reason to be upset over the incident with the sheriff. They had certainly appreciated Sandy's musical ability, and Hank told anyone who would pause to listen all about Allie's gift with cards.

"Regular little shark, she is," he would say, chuckling with pleasure. "Wish I still had a game going with some of the big old poker boys in town. I'd ring her in and wipe 'em out!"

All the McKinneys agreed that a child who could impress Hank Travis had to be someone extra special! J.T. said he remembered some of the men who used to play cards with Hank and that it would indeed be fun to let Allie loose on them. Not that it was likely to happen.

Of course, no one knew of the sweet kisses and private words Lynn and Sam had shared.

For which she was truly grateful. Had that become common knowledge, the teasing would have been far more intense, even embarrassing. Since she wasn't sure how she herself felt about him, she did not need kidding from the local "love experts." So she kept the kisses and the attraction to herself, even though she was at times tempted to talk to Cynthia or Ruth about them.

By Monday, however, Lynn felt it was time to get back into a serious routine. Her exchanges with Sam had given her renewed hope that he would agree with her plans and would be able to persuade the other investors to do likewise.

She decided to let Lightening work against a ranch horse with the reputation as a runner and a race winner. Jimmy Bolton, the cowboy who rode him regularly, was a competitive man, and she knew she'd get a good run out of them. Jim acted just delighted to get the chance to beat the "stuffin' outa that big horse," as he put it. Lynn asked if he wanted to put a little money down. He did, and soon the bunkhouse was a regular bookie spot with most of the cash being laid on the nose of the cow pony.

Lynn knew better, but she didn't bet more than ten dollars. It would have been like taking candy from babies!

The morning was a chilly one, and the ground was damp with dew, but Lightning was ready. When Lynn walked into the stable, he trumpeted eagerness, rather than just whinnying a welcome. She calmed him long enough to get the standard racing tack on him, but when she cinched the saddle, he blared a challenge. She hadn't put on the lightweight gear. He *knew* this was different. He knew he was to race this morning. This wasn't practice to him. This was war!

With a firm hand on the reins, she guided him down the path to the track where Jimmy and the cow pony waited. Once more, Lightning voiced a challenge, and she had to speak to him in stern tones in order to impress on him that such behavior wasn't appropriate for the racecourse. Lightning settled, but still Lynn could sense he was ready to fight as well as run.

That was something she knew she'd have to work on. A racehorse who wanted to kick and fight instead of win would be no good to himself or anyone else. She spoke softly but urgently to him, and finally he seemed ready to behave. Under her control, he moved into position on the track next to the other horse. Although his ears flicked, he did not try to move from her iron hand on the reins. Lynn began to focus on the race.

The makeshift bleachers were filled this morning with the cowhands who had put money on Jimmy. She scarcely noticed them. Ken Slattery, ranch foreman, who had agreed to be the starter, took his position. When he hollered, "Go!" they took off.

Lynn felt and heard nothing but Lightning. She rode low, pressed against his back and neck, her hands gripping the reins, but her will controlling him. He was a bullet from the gun of her mind, and she aimed him straight at the finish line. The smell of him filled her nostrils and the power that drove them both filled her heart.

They flew past Ken a second time and kept on going.

The results were gratifying. Lightning beat the pacing pony by so much distance that the match couldn't even be called a race. Jimmy and the other cowboys grumbled, but paid up good-naturedly. Lynn gave the money to Ken to put into a kitty for a crew barbecue later in the summer.

When she arrived at the kitchen for breakfast, she was feeling elated and confident. The future was going to work out, just the way she'd planned it.

"Hi, big brother," she said to Tyler, who was the only person still eating. She ruffled his hair as she passed him on the way to the coffeepot. "What're you doing today?" she asked.

"I have to go into Austin on some business," he replied.

"Oh. What kind of business?" Lynn poured coffee. There was an edge to her brother's voice that bothered her.

"Just business."

She came over and sat down at the table. "Tyler, is everything...uh, okay with you and Ruth? I don't mean to pry, but..."

His smile lit the morning. "Everything with me and Ruth is better than okay, little sis. It's the best!" He chuckled. "Better than the best, in fact." His expression sobered. "No, I'm not doing this for us. I'm doing it... I'm just doing it, okay?"

"Okay."

Tyler looked as if he was going to say something else then, but Hank appeared at the kitchen door, and whatever Tyler had thought of apparently went right out the window. The old man's face was gray, and he was holding his hand against one cheek. One eye was partly closed. He walked slowly, supporting himself heavily on his cane.

"Grandpa, are you all right?" Lynn got up, knocking over her chair and bringing Lettie Mae, who had been in the pantry, running to see what had happened. Lynn helped Hank into a chair that Tyler, equally concerned, pulled out.

"No, I ain't all right," Hank declared, his voice muffled. "I feel bad, and that's a fact."

"I'm calling Nate," Tyler said, running to the phone on the wall. "Does he have a fever?"

"I don't think so." Lynn felt her great-grandfather's forehead. "Actually seems cold. Clammy."

"He's got himself a toothache," Lettie Mae declared, standing back, folding her arms and regarding the old man. "I know the signs."

"You do, eh?" Hank glared at her. "Then whup me up something to help, woman!"

"Get him to that dentist friend of yours," Lettie Mae said to Lynn. "A man Hank's age that still has all his own teeth's bound to be losing some now and then."

"I ain't seeing no dentist," Hank stated. "Get me Doc Purdy, if you want. I'll see him." He grimaced and groaned. "I want some coffee. And don't go easy on the whiskey when you fetch it for me."

Lynn's heart ached. Her great-grandfather rarely showed pain openly. Usually, he just endured it silently or sat back in his rocking chair and drank whiskey until the pain gave way to the liquor. To hear him admit he needed a doctor was a sign of real trouble, she thought.

"He's got himself a real bad toothache," Lettie Mae insisted. "Lynn, girl, you ought to call that dentist man."

"Nate's on his way," Tyler said. "I'm going to tell Daddy." He left the kitchen.

"A good dentist is what he needs," Lettie Mae said again.

Hank, uncharacteristically, said nothing.

"I don't know, Lettie Mae." Lynn went to the cupboard and got out a bottle of Hank's "medicinal" whiskey. "Let's have Dr. Purdy take a look first." She filled a coffee mug half full of the hot liquid. The rest was reserved for the booze.

"Humph," said the cook.

"Pour generous, Lynnie," Hank muttered.

Lynn did. This was something she could do for her beloved, irascible great-grandfather.

For the rest of the morning, she stayed close to Hank, who had retired to his bedroom. When Dr. Purdy arrived, Lynn sat out on Hank's front porch, kicking her heels against the stone foundation. J.T., worried to the point of looking gray himself, stayed in Hank's room. Cynthia, who had been busy in the main house, came out of the kitchen door and called to Lynn. "Can you come up here for a minute?"

"I guess." Lynn got down and walked over the lawn that separated Hank's little house from the main one. She kicked at a tuft of grass that had heaved during the last frost.

"What is it?" she asked, coming through the screen door and letting it bang shut behind her. "I want to get back to Hank as soon as I..."

Her words trailed off as she focused on the kitchen table and as Cynthia gestured toward the two huge rose bouquets arranged there. "What?" Lynn stammered. "Who?"

"Your dentist," Lettie Mae said. "He sent one for you and one for us."

"It's a thank-you gift," Virginia explained. "The yellow ones, anyway. The other's for you. There's a card. Wasn't that thoughtful of the young man?"

"Oh, my," Lynn said.

Cynthia was all smiles. She bent over the arrangement of yellow rosebuds and baby's breath. "I am impressed," she said. "That Sam Russell has good, old-fashioned manners, Lynn." Then she stopped smiling. "How's Hank?"

"I don't know yet." Lynn walked over to the table. Her roses were pink. Peachy-pink, actually. A rare shade she knew must have cost Sam a bundle. There was a note attached. "Dr. Purdy hasn't finished with him yet," she added.

"The man needs a dentist, not a doctor." Lettie Mae stubbornly repeated her belief. "You call that Russell man and you thank him for the roses, and then you get him to see your great-grandpa, girl."

"I don't think I should." Lynn opened the envelope. "Not yet, anyway." She read the card.

Wednesday night? Call me.

"On the other hand . . ." she started to say.

Just then, Nate Purdy came through the kitchen door, J.T. behind him. "He's not in any real trouble," the doctor said before anyone could ask. "I gave him something for pain, and that, plus the booze he's put down already, ought to make him sleep awhile."

"What's wrong?" Lynn asked, setting the card aside. "I've never seen Hank like this."

Nate Purdy took the coffee that Lettie Mae handed him. "That's because you've never seen the man with a tooth that's about to—"

"I *told* you!" Lettie Mae declared. "I knew it was his teeth!"

"He's got a hell of an infection," Nate added. "The tooth'll have to be extracted, but not until the inflammation settles down. Now I've made out a prescription for antibiotics, and for pain medication until he can get treatment. I'll call Jan Foster right away. He's your family dentist, isn't he?"

"He is." J.T. sat down. "He can do it when Hank's ready."

"But Daddy, how about Sam?" Lynn asked. "I mean, Dr. Foster's just a regular dentist. Sam's kind of . . . well, more than that."

"Who's Sam?" Nate asked, regarding her as he sipped his coffee.

"Sam Russell." J.T. absently picked up the card Lynn had set down on the table. He looked at it, but was apparently not reading it. "He's a friend of Lynn's."

"He's an investor in my horse," Lynn added. "I met him last week, and—"

"Did he have a wife who died? A doctor named Marta Russell? Happened about five or six years back."

"That's him." Lynn glanced at her father.

J.T. was reading the card. "Say, Lynn. You didn't tell us you were seeing him socially."

Cynthia took the card from her husband. "Frankly, my dear," she drawled, "it's none of your business if she is."

"Heck, it's not." J.T. regarded Lynn. "She's my daughter. What about it, Lynn? I thought you two were business partners."

"Well, I—"

"If he's the man I think he is, you ought to seriously consider putting Hank in his care," Nate said, interrupting. "He's right on the cutting edge of dentistry, as I understand it. One who keeps up with the new developments and techniques might be just what Hank needs. All Jan Foster's liable to do is pull the tooth. It's traditional, and it's easier."

"Hank'd sure rather keep his teeth," J.T. commented, staring at the roses now. "He's had them this long. Seems wrong to haul 'em out after almost a hundred years of use." His face creased in a smile. "I'll talk to Russell about it. And Lynn, sorry to be nosy. Just looking after you, darlin'. That's all."

"I know, Daddy." Lynn got up and kissed him. "And I really don't mind. There's nothing between us, anyway. Just...friends."

"You know," Nate Purdy said, interjecting himself again into the conversation, "there're two sides to someone like this Russell. There's some as would say he was exploiting some of the new fashions in dentistry."

"What do you mean?" Lynn sat back down. So did her father. Out of the corner of her eye, Lynn saw Tyler come into the room. Her brother hadn't gone into town yet, since Hank had taken ill, but he'd spent most of the morning on the phone after the doctor arrived.

"I'm glad to hear it," he said, coming over and taking the last free chair. "You don't really know anything about the man."

Nate Purdy shrugged. "He's got a good reputation, but I've certainly heard some of the older, less innovative guys criticize what they refer to as his 'newfangled ideas.'"

"I see," said Tyler. He looked thoughtful. And worried. "Daddy, are you thinking about taking Grandpa to him?"

"Yes."

"I see," Tyler said again. He frowned and rubbed his face.

"While you all hash out Sam," Lynn said, suddenly angry and upset, though she wasn't exactly sure why, "I'm going to check on Grandpa." She took the card Sam had sent and stuck it in the pocket of her jeans.

"Where do you want the flowers, honey?" Virginia asked softly.

"In my room, please. Thanks, Virginia." And she left the kitchen, letting the screen door slam again.

Nate Purdy regarded the McKinneys. Then he looked at the door Lynn had just slammed. "Young'n got a beau in this dentist fellow?" he asked.

J.T. started to answer, but Tyler interrupted. "She says not," he said. "Maybe he's just a friend. But I'm going to check on him, anyway. She's involved with him because of the horse, and that makes us a little nervous. He may have some money invested in her racing, but she has a whole lot of herself. Just about all her hopes for the future are riding on that big black animal. So it's a matter of some concern to those of us that care about her."

Nate nodded. "I'm sure she appreciates your concern and takes your advice." He squinted, regarding J.T. "Which is more than I can say for some folks."

"What's that mean?" J.T. stared back.

"Means what're you doing sitting there sucking coffee when I told you in plain words to cut it out?"

"Hell you did! You told me . . ."

Rather than get involved in the ensuing argument, Tyler saluted Cynthia and left by the dining room door. He had no desire to listen to his father and the doctor go another round about J.T.'s health.

He still had an appointment in town.

HANK SLEPT the morning away and awoke demanding food. Soft food. While Lettie Mae and Virginia tended to his needs, Lynn called Sam's office. Sam's voice was warm. He sounded glad to hear from her.

"The roses are lovely," she said. "That was so nice of you. Cynthia is touched, let me tell you."

"And you? Have I managed to touch you?"

Lynn smiled. "Yes. I believe so. It was a thoughtful gesture."

"More than a gesture was meant in your case, believe me."

Lynn hesitated, not knowing how to respond. "I... About Wednesday night..."

"You can make it, can't you?"

"Of course. I wouldn't miss it. But I wondered, what do you have planned? I'd like an idea of what to wear."

"It's kind of a surprise, if you don't mind. I don't want to give it away." He laughed, the sound friendly and fun over the phone line. "Just wear a pretty dress and your smile, Lynn. That'll be enough for me."

"I think I can do that. Sam, there's something else I need to talk to you about. My—"

"The girls were hoping maybe they could see you before Wednesday," he said, interrupting her. "If it's not too much trouble, that is."

"Okay. I'll probably be in town tomorrow. When are they out of school?"

He told her, and Lynn promised to go by his house then and take the girls out for a treat. Sam thanked her and then had to get back to his patients. Lynn had no time to tell him about Hank. Oh, well, she thought. Plenty of time for that later.

CHAPTER EIGHT

IMMEDIATELY after speaking to Lynn and getting her promise that she would see the girls tomorrow afternoon, Sam called his home. He told Mrs. Findley to expect her visit. The housekeeper sounded surprised, but pleased. Sam hung up the phone and smiled. It was getting to be a time of surprises.

He'd promised Lynn a surprise, and that was what she was going to get. If she was going to continue being with the girls, she really did need to know about Sandy's extraordinary abilities. It was impossible to understand the sisters' relationship without grasping the younger one's potential and the pressures that brought to the whole family, himself included. So she thought Sandy played well when she was just sawing out country and western?

She had another think coming. And on Wednesday evening, she would get a chance to think it!

Furthermore, he owed her a lot more than a pleasant surprise. He couldn't believe how much better he already felt about the girls because of the brief time they'd spent with Lynn and her family.

The positive effects of that contact were already showing in their behavior.

On Sunday, in spite of being tired from the late night before, they had gotten up and gone to church with him without protest or griping. When they returned home, they'd done their chores and remaining homework. Conversation with them had been pleasant, good-natured and without conflict.

When he tried to get some insight from them about the change, however, they just shrugged and indicated that they had better things to do and think about than fussing or fighting. The only explanation Sam could come up with was that they felt better about themselves because the McKinneys all seemed to like them.

Well, he could understand that, couldn't he?

This morning, they had risen once more without making a federal case out of it, and both of them had gone off to school with good attitudes and obvious anticipation.

He was really looking forward to spending time with them this evening. They had been eager to share their experiences with their classmates, and he was now eager to get the details of their day.

Lynn was certainly just what the kids needed. His impulse to ask for her help had been absolutely on target! He was pleased with himself. And it didn't hurt that he was definitely attracted to her as well, though, of course, she was right about that part of their relationship having to take a back seat to other concerns.

Meanwhile, he owed her some work on his part of the bargain they had made. He had called the other two dentists earlier and had left messages for them to contact him when they were free for the day. He punched in the phone code for his financial advisor, Dean Fawcett, the man who had set him up with Phil and Dan and Lynn and the horse deal in the first place.

Time to talk.

ON THE OTHER SIDE of Austin, Tyler reached across a desk and shook the hand of the unusual private investigator Sheriff Wayne Jackson had recommended to him.

She hardly fit his idea of a hard-boiled detective. She looked more like a kindhearted grandmother. For certain, she would not have been his first choice. But during their discussion, she had struck him as levelheaded and competent. A real professional, in spite of her appearance.

"Thanks for taking the case, Ms. Morris," he said, smiling at the woman. She was plump, short and gray-haired. "I'll look forward to hearing from you."

"Mr. McKinney," Effie Morris said, "few people really look forward to hearing what a private investigator has to say." She reached over and took a small notebook from the side of her cluttered desk. "Usually, we confirm what the client suspects."

Tyler nodded. "That's what I'm afraid of. But you do what you have to. I need to know."

Effie Morris made a note in the book. "Let me ask you one more thing, Mr. McKinney."

"Sure. What?"

"How important is it that this Dr. Russell not know you're checking up on him? I don't need to know the reason you're doing it. That's entirely your affair. But if I had some idea of how much secrecy you need, I'd know how deep to dig."

"I'm afraid I don't exactly understand what you're saying."

Ms. Morris shrugged. "It's like this, you see. If I start looking into some of his business accounts, someone might let him know."

Tyler thought about it. "Well, I'd rather he didn't know. Unless you get on the trail of something important. Something that doesn't seem right about him." He frowned. "Then, I guess it doesn't matter."

"So you'd like me to use my own judgment."

"Yes, ma'am."

She smiled. "All right, Mr. McKinney. I'll do my best. I should have some results for your family fairly soon."

"DEAN." Sam was on the phone with his financial advisor. "Let me rephrase my question. If Lynn McKinney is right about her horse, the potential profit from letting her run him the way she wants is almost unlimited, isn't it?"

"It is, of course," Dean Fawcett replied. "I can't argue with that. But the odds—"

"Isn't that what this sort of investment is? Odds? A gamble?"

"Sure, Sam." The financial expert hesitated. "But the odds and the risk can be, um, arranged to the advantage of the investors. That's what—"

"You mean..."

"I mean that Phil and Dan are in a situation where immediate profit is important to them," Dean said. "I'm not giving away any secrets here. You're aware they're building a new clinic and need the money."

"Well, yes. I know about the clinic. In fact, they asked me to join their partnership a few months ago. I didn't, but not because I don't think they're good men. I prefer working on my own, and I just had too many other things going on in my life."

"Frankly, Sam, that makes you somewhat removed from their problems, doesn't it?"

"I suppose it might. I have put calls in to their offices and I plan to meet with them as soon as possible. I'm certainly willing to listen to their side of the situation."

"Sounds to me like your mind's made up."

"It may sound that way, but it's not."

Dean was quiet for a moment, then, "Sam, I can't emphasize enough the fact that Phil and Dan need money *now*. They're prepared to take legal action, if necessary, to get that horse out from under Ms. McKinney's control."

Sam's grip on the receiver tightened. "I don't think that drastic a step is necessary," he said, trying to keep his tone calm. "I think if we four just sit down together and talk, we—"

Dean cleared his throat. "I don't know if we have the time for that," he said. "Phil and Dan are upset enough to have fired her as trainer and jockey, as you know. I doubt they want to listen to her again. But it's worth a try. Sam, let me know what happens or if I can help in any way." He then changed the subject to discuss some of Sam's other investments.

By six that evening, Phil and Dan had not returned Sam's calls, and Sam went home, intending to call them after dinner. He entered his house with his mind on Lynn, Lightning and the future.

He heard the smooth sounds of Sandy's cello. He smiled, pleased she was practicing diligently in preparation for Wednesday night. He also heard Mrs. Findley in the kitchen. A wonderful aroma of dinner cooking wafted in the air. He relaxed, anticipating a very pleasant evening. Then he heard his housekeeper say, "Your father's home, Allison Russell. Come on out here and tell him what happened at school, young lady!"

The cello music suddenly turned sour.

"Alexandra Russell, you just keep on practicing!" Mrs. Findley scolded. "This isn't any of your business."

Sam's spirits sank. Mrs. Findley never used that tone to the girls or addressed them by their full names unless there was an extremely serious problem. The housekeeper was a notoriously soft touch when it came to the children, so if she was that upset, the disaster must be of mammoth proportions. He went into the kitchen.

Allie slunk in from the hall. She didn't look at either adult, as she took a seat at the kitchen table and stared in silence at the tabletop. Sam set down his briefcase on the counter and sat opposite her. Mrs. Findley turned her back to them, apparently satisfied that her job was done. She had set up the parent-child conference.

"Evening, Allie," Sam said. "What's up, honey?"

"Um." Allie continued to study the tabletop. "Not much."

"Allison, what happened today? Did something go wrong at school?"

"Um. Nothing, Daddy."

"Show him the note," Mrs. Findley's back said.

"Note?" Sam raised questioning eyebrows.

She sighed, shrugged, sullen and reluctant. "I got in a little trouble. That's all."

"I see. What note?"

"It's on the counter next to the mail," Mrs. Findley said. "Allison, get it for your father."

Allie rose slowly, as if every molecule of her body was protesting. She went over to the pile of mail, sorted through it and took out an envelope. She handed it to her father and went back to her seat without saying a word.

Sam took out the letter and read it. He reread it. He laid the letter and envelope on the table and looked at Allie.

"We have a problem, honey," he said. His tone reflected the sympathy he felt.

His daughter looked up at him.

Sam tapped the paper. "Your teacher says you hit one of your classmates."

Allie almost smiled. "That's right," she said. "I told what happened at the ranch—about how I won the gold coins in a card game—and everybody said I was fibbing! Even Mrs. Chambers didn't believe me."

Sam rested his chin on his hand and regarded his daughter. "I can tell her you weren't lying."

"Oh, Daddy! Please! Tell her she's a big . . ."

"Hold it, honey. I agree you were telling the truth. But you were wrong to do what you did. Here in the note, you teacher says that you jumped up out of your chair, turned over another child's desk and started hitting her." He tapped the paper again. "And I don't think Mrs. Chambers is lying about that."

Allie ducked her head, turned red and bit her lip.

"Is she?"

"No."

"No? Then what are you going to do about it?"

Allie shook her head, tears forming. "I . . . I don't know, Daddy. But I wasn't lying!" She looked up at him, angry and defiant despite the tears.

He was suddenly reminded of Lynn.

"You weren't lying, but you were hitting," he said.

"It wasn't her fault!" Sandy appeared in the doorway. "During recess, I got pushed for saying I saw a horse that was going to win the Kentucky Derby and a man who was almost a hundred years old!"

Sam stared. Sandy sported a bruise on her cheek-bone near her eye. "Honey!" He hurried over to her. "What in the world . . . ?" He held her face tenderly and examined the injury.

"She's all right," Mrs. Findley said, finally turning around and joining the discussion. "I took her to Dr. Lambert the moment she arrived home like that. He said it would look ugly for a while, but it's nothing serious."

"How....? Why?" Sam was at a complete loss.

"She got shoved, just like she said," Allie said, tense and angry. "Only she didn't get a note for home because she didn't hit back."

"I didn't have a chance." Sandy pulled away from her father. "I would have, though!" She scowled, carefully so as not to aggravate the bruise on her face. "I would have beat Cindy Weaver to a pulp! If that teacher hadn't come along and stopped us fighting, I could have—"

"That's enough of that kind of talk! Bragging and fighting are just not the way a Russell behaves!"

"But, Daddy—"

"I said that's enough. Now, we are going to sit down to the good dinner that Mrs. Findley fixed for us. We're going to eat it. And then we are going to have a family conference and decide what needs to be done about this situation. Is that clearly understood by everyone?"

The girls nodded.

Sam decided to drop the subject for now. He detected a strong note of sullen defiance in their tones and the keen glint of anger in their eyes. It hurt him. Lord, but he hated to be the heavy all the time!

But there was no one else to take the role. And he loved these children too much not to do the best possible job he could. Even when it meant appearing mean in order to make sure they learned the lessons they needed. As Mrs. Findley prepared to serve dinner, he made one last announcement.

"Always remember," he said, his tone soft and gentle, "that I love you more than anything else in the world. If I seem tough, it's only because I care so much about you."

The girls' eyes filled with tears, but they said nothing.

Sam felt rotten, but he knew he was right. Still, the feeling was not pleasant. Not pleasant at all.

LYNN WAS IN AUSTIN early on Tuesday with Beverly Townsend to look for a dress to wear for her date with Sam the following evening. She'd made the mistake of confiding in Beverly. Once she knew the details, Beverly had insisted on helping out and absolutely refused to take no for an answer.

"It sounds to me like this man is getting to be kind of important to you," she said. "And Lynn, honey, you are going to knock his socks off, if I have anything to do with it!"

"I do like him, but it's no more than that."

"I hear romance. Don't tell me I don't!"

"You're jumping the gun, Beverly. I just want to look nice."

"You just hush. I'll handle everything. Sam Russell will take one look at you and the man won't know what hit him."

By lunch they had hit all the main malls. Because Lynn was so petite, the pickings were slim. While they took a lunch break, Beverly commiserated.

"It's a darn ol' shame they don't make enough clothes for small women like you," she said. "If I was in charge, of course, they would."

That made Lynn laugh.

But when Beverly started inquiring about other matters, she didn't find it so funny.

"So, this Sammy Russell has himself two little girls who think you walk two inches off the floor, does he? And they love your family, too, of course."

Lynn described Allie and Sandy. "They do like the family," she said. "I don't think they have many relatives of their own, and they did have fun on Saturday. As for me and them, we get along," she added. "That's all there is to it."

"Well, that's enough for many folks." Beverly picked thoughtfully at her salad. "Lynn, just how serious is this with you and—"

"It is not serious at all!" Lynn raised her right hand. "I swear. Honestly, I just met the man. We . . . well, there are sparks, but . . ."

"But I've never seen you blush like this when you denied you were interested in any of those little ol' boys who used to hang around you when we were in school. Hmmm?" Beverly smiled. "Honey, you are not telling me the whole, entire truth."

Lynn couldn't meet her cousin's gaze directly. "Maybe it's because I don't know the whole, entire truth yet myself."

They did finally locate a shop with a selection that delighted Beverly. She made Lynn try on a dozen outfits before choosing two. "Those will do you nicely for almost any occasion," she declared. "Not just an evening out."

"But which one?" Lynn looked at them both. One was a dressy suit, with a short skirt, a jacket and a frilly blouse. The dark green color did interesting things to her eyes. Beverly told her the material was gabardine wool and of the finest quality. The other was a navy-blue silk dress with a longer skirt. It was cut in a way to show off her narrow waist, and the salesclerk had oohed and aahed over that.

"Both," said Beverly. "They're perfect."

"But I can't afford to buy both."

"You can't afford not to. If this man is smart, you'll be needing nice things to wear while he courts you, honey. Trust me."

Courts me? Was that what she wanted? Well, maybe. She bowed to Beverly's greater experience in these matters and took both outfits.

They got to the Russell house an hour or so after the girls arrived home from school. Beverly's Cadillac was not out of place here, Lynn thought. The house was quite imposing. It had a New Orleans-y look to it, she decided. It was a white stucco structure adorned with fancyworked iron and surrounded by trees and shrubbery.

"Your Sam lives here?" Beverly seemed impressed, too. "Nice. Nice. My, my. Lynnie, you do pick 'em."

"I haven't picked anyone," Lynn said, a little annoyed. She opened the passenger door and got out. "Nor has anyone picked—"

"Lynn! Yeaaaaay!"

"You came! You really came!"

Sandy and Allie came racing out the front door, their arms outstretched, ready to hug her. Their faces were so full of delight to see her that Lynn was deeply moved.

Then she saw the bruise on Sandy's cheek. "What happened, honey!" she cried. "How did you get hurt?"

Sandy shrugged, but she didn't say anything.

"Somebody hit her at school," Allie answered for her sister. "And I got in a fight in class. But I didn't get hit. I'm teaching Sandy how to defend herself now."

"Oh, I remember what school could be like," Lynn said. "You do have to learn to take care of yourself. Come here, both of you and give me a hug!" After she greeted them enthusiastically, she introduced Beverly.

"Are you a movie star?" Sandy asked. "Is that really your car? You're beautiful."

"No, she's not a movie star, dummy," Allie said. "She's Lynn's cousin."

"Beverly's lots of wonderful things, but she's not a movie star," Lynn replied. "She can shop like one, though. That's what we did all this morning and most of the afternoon. I needed some new clothes. Since I don't have to dress up to ride Lightning unless we're racing, I don't have many things to wear besides jeans. Usually, that's what I prefer anyway."

Sandy piped up, "Maybe I ought to be a lady jockey like you. Then I wouldn't have to worry about what I wear."

"You don't have to *worry*, darlin'," Beverly said. "Wearing nice clothes is supposed to be *fun.*"

"Lynn doesn't think so, do you?" Allie asked.

"Beverly is changing that for me. She can outfit anybody. I'm living proof."

"Can you?" Allie regarded Beverly skeptically. "Could you help me? I need some new clothes." She glanced at her little sister. "Sandy does, too."

Beverly beamed. "Well, why don't we talk about it, then we'll see what your daddy wants to do."

A shadow came over both girls at the mention of their father.

"Daddy's just a man. He doesn't know what girls' clothes are," Sandy said. "Come inside and meet Mrs. Findley. We're supposed to go shopping with her tomorrow and get some new clothes. Daddy gave her some money for it this morning." Sandy hesitated. "But she's kind of old and doesn't know what's 'in.'"

"If you know what we mean," Allie added.

"Why, I do believe I do," Beverly said. She regarded the girls' outfits critically. "Your clothes are lovely, but sort of, well, uninteresting." Pause. "If you know what *I* mean."

Laughter.

"And," Beverly said, "you are both so pretty." She considered the children with a critical expression. "Let's see. In the color system, I'll bet you're a cool summer, Sandy. And Allie, why, I do believe you're a warm winter. Isn't that great?"

"Why?" The girls both asked the question.

"Well, it means you can share a lot of your clothes. Not all, but a lot. That means you can buy more, since it'll all go double!" She lowered her voice. "And your daddy won't mind so much." The three of them giggled like conspirators.

Lynn enjoyed the moment. This was obviously a meeting made in heaven, she thought as they went inside.

The girls introduced Beverly and Lynn to Mrs. Findley, who greeted them warmly. An awkward moment occurred when the housekeeper reminded the girls of something they were supposed to do—a kind of punishment for the playground fracas. But Sandy and Allie insisted they had already performed that chore and were free to go.

Mrs. Findley smiled. "Well, your father did say yesterday that he wanted you both to spend some time with Miss McKinney today, so I suppose it's all right." She turned to Beverly. "And if you can help them find nice clothes, I would be grateful. Shopping with them is almost too much for me these days. Their sizes are changing so quickly, and they're so *particular*. Things have to be a certain style, whatever the other children are wearing and things like that. I just can't keep track of fashion, I suppose."

"Believe me, Mrs. Findley, I understand." Beverly studied Sandy's face. "And I think we can do more than shop," she said. "I think it might be time to show you how to use a little makeup to cover those bruises on your face until they fade, darlin'.''

"Makeup?" Sandy's eyes widened. "For me?"

"Sure." Beverly drew her in for a hug. "Just a little cover-up." She looked at Allie. "And maybe a teeny bit of lip color for both of you."

Lynn caught Mrs. Findley's look of concern. "Don't worry," she told the older woman, "I'll take full responsibility."

CHAPTER NINE

SAM GOT IN very late that night. He had intended to make it a short day at the office and to get home early in order to continue dealing with the girls' discipline problem, but two emergency patients late in the day put an end to that plan. It was close to eleven o'clock by the time he put the key into the lock on the side door.

Mrs. Findley greeted him. She had been catching a nap, she confessed. "The children are asleep," she said. "Clean worn out from the shopping trip those young women took."

"Women? Shopping trip?" Sam set down his briefcase on the kitchen table and went over to the refrigerator to get out a beer. "Oh, yes. My mind seems to be anywhere but here, today. You know, I completely forgot Lynn was coming over."

Mrs. Findley beamed. "Well, she did. And she brought along her cousin, Miss Beverly Townsend. You know she was a beauty queen a few years back. My, she is so lovely. And the girls just had a grand time with them."

"Lynn McKinney has a cousin who's a beauty queen?" Sam took out a beer and opened it. "Hard to imagine." He took a swallow, then thought about what he had said. "Not that Lynn's not beautiful," he added, as much to himself as to Mrs. Findley. "It's just that she's not the beauty-queen type, if you know what I mean."

"Well, they don't look much alike. That McKinney lady is hardly taller than Allie, and pretty and sweet enough but kind of ordinary next to Miss Townsend." Mrs. Findley shrugged. "But the girls really do think a lot of her." She paused, gauging his mood. "She certainly did do a good job of lifting them out of the blues over that school problem."

"Good."

"They wrote the letters. Do you want to take a look at them?"

"Later." Sam rubbed his eyes. "Are they on my desk?"

"Yes. I made sure everything was done before I let them take off. It was all right to let them go out, I hope. You did say that once they'd written the apologies, they were free to do what they wanted. I tried calling you to check, but I was told you were at the hospital in surgery."

"I know." Sam drank. "Two emergencies. Sorry to be so late but it couldn't be helped."

"No problem." She gathered up her belongings. "Tonight was no trouble at all. They were out until almost ten. I had the house to myself most of the evening."

"Ten? Did you say ten?" Sam set down the beer. "Mrs. Findley, it's a school night."

"I know that. They did write those letters, though, as I told you. I saw them working. The dears were just pouring out their hearts on paper. It was not easy for them. I thought they deserved the outing."

"But *ten* o'clock!"

"Oh, you know girls when they're shopping. They said the time just got away from them."

"I see." Actually, Sam had no idea about girls and shopping and how time could get away from them. He just knew another of his rules had bitten the dust.

"And the stuff they bought! My goodness. Well, you let me know when you expect the Goodwill collection people, because both children have emptied their closets of their old things and we packed it all out in the garage."

"What?"

"Miss McKinney and Miss Townsend said it was the best thing to do. And I agree. Those clothes were getting too small or too shabby for your daughters. I can say that without hesitation. They have not looked their best lately."

"You can? Well..." Sam stopped. Shut his eyes. Counted to ten. "All right, Mrs. Findley. Sorry. I'm tired, and I didn't expect to come home to a rummage sale. Don't worry about it. I'll take care of it."

"I wasn't worried." She smiled. "Those young women were just wonderful to the girls. You should be grateful. Good night, Doctor."

"Good night, Mrs. Findley."

After the housekeeper left, Sam stayed in the kitchen for a while, unwinding and thinking. Not only about his daughters and Lynn, but also about Lynn and Lightning.

One of the many phone calls he'd had that day had been from Phil. He and Dan wanted to meet and talk about the problems they were having with Lynn. Sam had agreed to a luncheon conference on Friday, the earliest all of them could get together.

Friday. Sam finished his beer. A lot could happen between now and Friday. He rinsed the bottle and set it in the glass recycling container. Then he went to see his children.

They were both sound asleep. He bent and kissed them, and felt so much love, his eyes watered. But they slept on. Not even Allie, who was a relatively light sleeper, stirred when he went over and turned on the light in the closet to inspect the new purchases. Good Lord, he thought, they've spent the budget for the next ten years. Sam Russell wasn't sure whether he should be furious, or grateful, as Mrs. Findley suggested.

So he just laughed. At himself, mostly. He had asked for this when he asked Lynn to be a friend to his girls.

He had no business getting angry about it.

He checked the sleepers once more, then went into his den to read the letters they had written.

After dinner last night Allie and Sandy had agreed to write a detailed description of their Saturday experience at the ranch, explain why they had not been able to control their reactions when accused of lying and finally apologize for their behavior. Sam phoned both teachers, and both said the arrangement was satisfactory.

Mrs. Chambers, Allie's teacher, had been particularly reasonable, confessing that she, too, had thought the child was inventing the story. Sam had little trouble convincing the woman of the truth, however. The girls really had spent time with a woman who rode a racehorse, and Allie actually had won gold coins in a poker game with a ninety-nine-year-old man.

Last night Sam had been satisfied that life would now begin to return to normal.

After reading his daughters' literary works, however, he knew it had a long way to go! Though they had done what they were told, a strong element of defiance was easy to read between the lines.

The following morning, he expected the girls to be tired and crabby. To his amazement, they bounced up at first call, bright and eager to try on their new finery. He had to admit that it had been worth every penny when they came out to breakfast. They looked sharp, stylish, smart and pretty as pictures.

Pictures that were smiling, not scowling or pouting as so often lately.

Given their good mood, he decided to wait to question them about the content of their ''apologies.''

''So,'' he said, sliding waffles onto their plates, ''you two had a good time yesterday with Lynn and her cousin, uh, what's her name?''

''Beverly.'' Sandy speared a sausage. ''Townsend. She lives on a ranch, too. But she's not crazy about horses like Lynn is. She says you get too dirty and smelly, messing with horses. She's a beauty queen.''

''Was. She quit.'' Allie poured syrup on her waffle. ''She's still real pretty, but she wants to do something else with her life.''

''Like what?'' Sam sipped coffee.

Allie shrugged. ''She says she's not sure yet.''

''I know what I want to do,'' Sandy said, her face bent over her breakfast.

"What's that?"

"Ride horses. I don't want to play the cello anymore."

Sam put down his coffee cup slowly. "What's made you change your mind, honey?" he asked.

As if he didn't know.

"If I ride horses, I don't have to worry about people laughing at me."

Sam was puzzled. "I don't get it, honey. What does riding horses, playing the cello and being laughed at have to do with... Wait just a minute, here. Are you wearing makeup?"

"Beverly said—"

"I don't care what anyone said! You're too young to be wearing makeup." Sam looked at Allie. "You, too?"

"It's just—"

"Both of you get into the bathroom and wash that stuff off!"

"Daddy, no! The kids will laugh at me."

"I don't care about the kids. I'm your father. I'm telling you, no makeup. Wash it off. Now!"

They both scurried from the kitchen. Sam heard them weeping as they washed their faces. He had probably been too harsh, but it was too late to take it back. If he did, they'd try to get away with more next time.

He'd have to put an end to it right now.

"LYNN, PHONE," Virginia Parks called from the kitchen door. "I think it's Sam."

Lynn hurried in from the backyard. She had been working with Cynthia out in the big rose garden behind the swimming pool. "Thanks," she said to the housekeeper and took the phone. "Hello."

"What are you doing to my kids!"

"Sam?"

"Who do you think this is? My daughters both had makeup on this morning!"

Lynn clenched the receiver. "Sam, calm down."

"I will not! They had makeup on their faces, and Sandy says she wants to ride horses, not play the cello! Lynn, this is way out of hand, as far as I'm concerned!"

"It's not my fault."

"Then who the hell's fault—"

"Yours! You asked me to be friends with your kids. You asked me to show them the ranch. You asked me to come by yesterday and visit. You... you... you..." She ran out of words.

Silence on the other end.

"Sam, you asked me to befriend them. To show them my world. Well, that includes makeup and horse riding."

Silence.

"Sam, are you all right?"

"No." He sounded so tired. Defeated, almost.

"Sam, are the girls all right? They told me about the fighting."

"They're all right. But the letters they wrote to their teachers, the makeup, the new clothes, the announcement Sandy didn't want to play anymore..."

"Sam, she doesn't mean it."

"She's never said anything like this before. Lynn, I know it was my idea to involve you with them in the first place, but maybe it was a bad idea. Maybe you..."

She clenched the receiver tighter. "Maybe I'm a bad influence? Is that what you're saying?"

"No, I...Well, I... Well, maybe you are."

"Goodbye, Sam."

"Wait, I didn't mean that the way it sounded. I mean maybe they need a woman who's a little more..."

"A little more what, Sam? Come on, spit it out!"

"All right. A little more of a lady. Less... I don't know...tough. Allie said you encouraged her to teach Sandy how to hit back so she wouldn't end up with a black eye next time."

"And what's wrong with that?"

"There shouldn't *be* a next time! I've raised them to be—"

"You've raised them to be great kids, Sam Russell. And they're going to be great young women. I'm sorry you have such a narrow point of view that you can't see that. Goodbye.'' Lynn hung up, her hand tingling from the pressure of holding on to the receiver with such a tight grip. ''And good riddance,'' she added.

She turned her back and headed out the door, ignoring the puzzled expressions on Virginia's and Lettie Mae's faces.

As she slammed the door, the phone rang again. ''I'm not here,'' she yelled over her shoulder.

She stomped across the yard, past the swimming pool and out to the rose garden. She went through the gate, slamming it shut, too.

Cynthia looked up from her pruning. ''Was that Sam?'' she asked. ''You don't look particularly happy.''

''It was Sam.'' Lynn pulled on her gardening gloves and picked up her shears. ''And no, I'm not happy.''

''Want to tell me?''

Lynn snapped the shears at a thorny stem. ''No.''

''Is he being a jerk about his kids?''

''Um-hmm.'' Lynn pruned, then looked up. ''How did you know?''

''I think he's a little jealous of the affection they have for you. Confused by it, too, if I don't miss my guess.''

"What?" Lynn stood up. "That's crazy." She pushed her hair back. "He's the one who asked me to get friendly with them. It wasn't my idea, it was his!"

"All the more reason it might upset him that it's happening."

"I don't get it. I don't get it at all."

"I can't say I do, either," Cynthia admitted. "But remember that this man has raised his daughters alone for five years. He's not shared them with anyone."

"So that makes him unique?"

"What exactly did he say?"

Lynn shrugged. "He was pretty upset. About the makeup Beverly bought them."

"Makeup?"

Lynn explained about the black eye and the fighting. "He made some remark about my not being ladylike enough for them," she added.

"Gosh. I can't imagine that."

Lynn had to smile. "Don't be sarcastic, Cynthia. He has some strange ideas about what a lady is. His kids are plenty ladylike and polite. What they need is someone to help them have... I don't know. Have more..."

"Fun?"

Lynn shrugged. "Maybe. Anyway, they sure enjoyed being out with us yesterday. I can't believe he'd get so hot over a little cover-up and lip gloss."

"Maybe that's not what's upsetting him."

"What, then?"

"I think you need to ask him yourself."

"I hung up on him."

"Call back."

Lynn was about to retort in the negative, but something made her pause. "You really think he might be jealous of me?"

"I think so. Remember how jealous you and your brothers were of me?"

"Oh. Yeah."

"Call him back, Lynn. If he means anything to you at all. Even if just the kids mean anything to you. Call him. You owe yourself, if no one else."

Lynn thought. "You're right," she said. "Thanks, Cynthia. I needed to hear that."

This time when she called, she used the upstairs phone, figuring she'd have more privacy.

But Sam was neither at home nor at his office.

Lynn spoke to Mrs. Williams. "Any idea when he's coming in?" she asked.

"I honestly don't know," the receptionist admitted. "He called in to cancel all his appointments early this morning. Said he had some trouble with his children that he had to take care of at their school."

"I see." Lynn thought. "He cancelled *all* his appointments you say?"

"Well, no, not all of them. Just this morning's. He said he'd let me know about the later ones. They're both up at the hospital. He did some emergency work there last night."

"What hospital?"

Mrs. Williams told her. In fact, she told Lynn enough to make her begin to understand some of the pressures on Sam Russell. Some of the reasons why he'd blown up over what was a relatively insignificant issue with his children. After she hung up, she sat in her room for a long time and thought about Sam and what Cynthia had said about him.

Then she made a decision.

SAM CAME OUT of the hospital late that afternoon. He was tired and still upset about his argument with Lynn. It was not until he was halfway across the parking lot that he noticed someone sitting in the passenger seat of his Subaru. He quickened his pace, alarm fading to anger then to astonishment when he realized who it was. He opened his door and said, "What are you doing here, Lynn?"

"Good evening to you, too," she said, smiling. "We have a date tonight."

"I thought . . ." Sam paused. "You look . . ."

"What, Sam?"

"You look great." He tossed his briefcase and bag into the back seat and got in. "But I thought you were too mad at me to keep our date."

"Oh, I am mad. I think you're being unfair and more than a bit pigheaded when it comes to the girls."

"Then why...?"

"Sam Russell, you asked me to help you, and I intend to keep my part of that bargain. What's bugging me is that we struck a deal on Friday in your office. And then on Saturday, I thought we...well, that we had a little more than a business deal going between us. You sent me flowers. Asked me to see the girls again yesterday. Asked me out for tonight. Now, you seem to want to act as if none of that happened."

"That's ridiculous!" His hands gripped the steering wheel. "Of course it all happened. I'm just not sure it should have."

"Why?"

"I don't know if it's right, that's all."

"How will we ever know if we won't try?"

"Lynn, I..."

"Sam, don't say anything else about us. Not now. Let's stick to the kids and the horse, okay?"

"Fine with me."

"Good, how are things going at home?"

Sam looked at her. She was so tiny. Almost smaller than Allie. But dressed in that attractive green suit, her hair curled into an auburn cloud around her face, jewelry and . . . yes, even makeup on, she was clearly all woman. Her body might be small, but her spirit was not and her presence seemed to fill the car.

"Okay, I . . ." His voice stuck for a second. Sam cleared his throat, his senses suddenly very alert to her. "How . . ." His voice caught. He cleared his throat again. "How did you get into my car? I always lock it."

"I figured you would." She held up a key. "I also figured you were the type to have a spare attached by a magnet to the underside somewhere." She tossed the key in the air and caught it. "I was right." She patted her knees. "Had a heck of a time getting at it without ripping up my panty hose," she added ruefully. "Jeans are definitely better for breaking and entering, let me be the first to tell you!"

Sam laughed—softly at first then louder and louder. Lynn watched him in alarm as he lapsed into uncontrollable mirth.

"Are you all right?" she asked, rolling down the window on her side and fanning air across to him. "Sam, speak to me! Please!"

Sam wiped his eyes. "Yes, I'm all right. I'm fine. What is it about you, Lynn McKinney? What is it that you're doing to me and my family?'' He settled back and regarded her.

"I don't... I'm not trying..." She couldn't finish her protest. She *was* trying. She wanted so much from this man. So many things, selfish and unselfish. She hardly knew where to begin.

Sam was serious now. "I was all prepared to say our deal concerning the kids was off. Of course, I still intend to meet with Phil and Dan. We all need to protect our investment. Is that why you came here?"

"Not exactly. I came because I care about the girls and I... I thought you deserved a chance to explain."

"Oh, you did, did you? Explain what?"

"Well." She sat back and smoothed her skirt. "Like why the girls really got into fights, for instance. And why putting a little cover-up on a bruise automatically makes your daughter a painted lady."

"I didn't say that."

"The tone of your voice implied it. I expect she was crushed."

Sam sighed, sober again. "Well, she wasn't happy. You're right, I guess. Maybe I did overreact."

"Sam." She reached over and touched his hand. "How are your patients doing?"

"Um. Better. The boy needed to have his tooth regrafted. I think he'll be fine. The woman was badly injured in a car accident. But it looks like she will pull through, thank goodness.''

"I'm so glad to hear that.''

He slumped a little in the seat. ''In my profession I don't often get involved with life-and-death situations.'' He rubbed his forehead, then his closed eyes. ''I'm afraid it makes me less than pleasant to be around.''

"Sam, I understand. I don't say I like it, but I think I do understand.''

"Thanks.'' He reached over and touched her hand, briefly.

"Speaking of patients, we have one at home. My great-grandfather is having some problems with a tooth.''

"Want me to take a look at him?'' Sam sat up, his careworn expression fading, his look intent.

"Yes. But not yet. He's under Dr. Purdy's care.''

"Antibiotics? To reduce the infection and swelling?''

"Yes.''

Sam sat back. ''I hope to goodness no one yanks the tooth before I get a look at it. At Mr. Travis's age, what dentition he has left should be treated with great respect.''

"I agree. I put my two cents in for you as a consultant. But it is up to my father and Hank.''

Sam's smile was wide and sudden. "Quite right, it is." He covered her hand with his. "You're a special person, Lynn," he said. "I think I'm just beginning to find out how special."

Warmth spread through her. "So are you, Sam. That's really why I came tonight. What were we going to do on our date?"

"Um." He glanced down at her hand. "We are...that is, Sandy is—was going to play a concert. I don't know now if she still is."

"Have you talked to her since this morning?" She stroked a fingertip over his knuckles.

"No." He turned his hand over and caught hers in a gentle grip. "I did see her, though. I spent a while at their school. I was unhappy with the letters of apology they wrote. I wanted to see if there was more to the incidents than I had been told."

"I thought they just had a couple of tussles with other kids. Why did you have to—"

"Lynn." He took his hand away. "You can't just make assumptions about my kids. You've got to know all the facts. Allie bragged in class about winning the gold coins from Hank, and then she jumped on another child when the child challenged her."

"Why—?"

"Let me finish! Sandy was pushed by another girl when she—"

"I don't care why the girls got into fights, Sam. What I want to know is why you're so upset about it."

He turned to face her, astonishment in his eyes. "What? Why I'm upset? Why in the world shouldn't I be upset? My daughters' behavior has never—"

"Sam, haven't they been in trouble in school before? Surely this isn't the first time they've had a spat in the playground and come home with a bruise?"

He seemed to draw into himself. "Yes, it is."

"Oh."

He settled back. "It is, and although I know you aren't to blame, I—"

"Hold it! I won't even consider taking any credit for their standing up for their rights. You taught them that, and if you can't see that, I don't know if you're capable of understanding anything!"

"Thanks a lot!"

They sat in angry silence for a moment.

Then Sam said, "Where's your car?"

"I was dropped off."

"Well, wasn't that clever. Now I suppose I have to take you home."

"No. I can always call the ranch and have someone drive into town to pick me up. But I'm not going to leave until we work out this mess."

"Why?"

Lynn didn't look at him. "I'm not sure," she said softly. "Maybe I think the girls deserve a little better deal than they're getting. Maybe..."

"Maybe what?"

"Sam, I don't know." She turned to face him. "I can't honestly tell you why I bothered to get all dressed up, have Ken drive me here, break into your car and wait for almost an hour for you, only to be yelled at and insulted."

"I haven't—"

"Oh, yes, you have! You've said I'm not a fit companion for your daughters. That it's my fault they're acting the way they are. Sam, I've been with them, what, a few hours of their lives? You've been around always. Figure out who's really responsible for their behavior!"

"If it's me, then why all of a sudden...?" He broke off, and covered his eyes with a hand.

Lynn noticed that his hand was trembling. She waited.

"Lynn," he said, "I don't want to fight with you. I don't want to fight with anyone. I can't understand what's happening with my children. I'm not sure about my own feelings these days. I'm sorry to take it out on you."

"Okay. Apology accepted."

He took his hand away from his face and gazed at her. "You really do look pretty this evening."

"Thanks. I believe my cousin is more than partly responsible. She took me shopping yesterday."

"And took my daughters shopping, also." His smile was wry, but at least he was smiling.

"Do you mind so very much? They did need new clothes."

"They did. And I really don't mind. It was just kind of a shock. They looked terrific this morning, and until I stirred up the pot by reacting to the makeup, they were in a good mood."

He held on to the steering wheel. "Lynn, can we start over with all this?"

"I'd like to give it a try."

Sam smiled as he started the car.

They drove to his home and went inside through the garage door entry. Lynn tensed as they entered the kitchen, anticipating a confrontation between father and daughters. But no one was there. She looked at Sam. He didn't seem too alarmed.

"Allie? Sandy?"

"Out here, Daddy."

"In the backyard, Doctor."

The voices, Mrs. Findley's and Allie's, came through the opened sliding-glass doorway in the living room. Sam led Lynn in that direction.

The housekeeper and Sam's older daughter were outside. Allie brightened when she saw Lynn, but she didn't run over to her as she had the afternoon before. She wore an old pair of cut-off jeans and a T-shirt.

"Where's Sandy?" Sam asked.

Mrs. Findley stood up, wiping her brow and getting more dirt on her face. "She's lying down in her room," she said. "She has an upset tummy, she says."

"I see." Sam stood still and put his hands in his pockets. "So she won't be playing the concert tonight?"

Mrs. Findley shook her head slowly.

Allie looked down at the ground.

Lynn put her hand on Sam's arm. "Mind if I talk to her?"

"Go ahead. I don't know what difference it'll make, but you're welcome to try."

"Sam, she may really be sick."

"Sure." He sounded defeated. Almost indifferent. "Go ahead, if you want."

Lynn looked at Allie. The girl met her glance briefly, pleadingly.

Wondering about that, Lynn went into the house.

Sandy was on her bed in the room she shared with her sister. The little girl lay on her back, with her hands behind her head. She stared at the ceiling. She did not look over when Lynn entered the room.

"Not feeling so hot?" Lynn asked.

Sandy regarded her. "Hey," she said, almost smiling, "what're you doing here?"

Lynn went over and sat on the other bed. "I thought I was going to get to hear you play tonight. I guess not, though."

Sandy sat up. "My tummy hurts." She placed her small hand on her midsection. "It really does." She grimaced.

"I'm sorry."

"Where's Daddy?"

"Outside, I think."

"Is he mad at me?" Sandy's tone dropped to a whisper.

"Of course not."

"Are you?"

"Not at all. Why should I be?"

Sandy lay back down. "Maybe because I'm not really sick." She stared up at the ceiling.

Lynn smiled. "I think what you have is a case of the butterflies."

"Uh-huh."

"Is that a yes uh-huh or a no uh-huh?"

Sandy sat back up. "Do you really want to hear me play?"

"Sure do."

"You heard me the other night at your house."

Lynn shrugged. "Your daddy says that wasn't what you usually do. I guess I'm just curious."

Sandy regarded her for a moment. Then she swung her legs over the side of the bed and stared at the floor. "What if I stay feeling sick? What if I throw up on stage?"

Lynn didn't laugh. "Try not to think about it. If you feel really bad you can go backstage. But you'll probably be fine. I know sometimes when I'm in a race I feel sick in the beginning, but it goes away."

The little girl sat up. "I thought grown-ups never got scared. And how come they always think they know everything?"

"I think it's because we've lived longer so we've seen more and we're better at knowing what's going on. That's all."

Sandy considered that. "But why do you get to tell us what to do all the time?"

Lynn shrugged. "Got me," she confessed. "I'm over twenty-one and my father and big brothers still try to tell me what to do all the time."

"They do?" Her eyes widened. "But you're big!"

"Not as big as they are!" Lynn held one hand high above her head. "And in a few years, you're going to be bigger than me, too, because I'm so short. But don't you go trying to tell me what to do, kid!" She balled her fist and made a fierce face.

Sandy laughed. Lynn laughed. Then Sandy sprang off her bed and ended up hugging Lynn. "I feel so much better now. I'll play for you," she said. "And I won't throw up!"

CHAPTER TEN

THE CONCERT WAS at eight. They had time for a quick supper before they left the house. Because she had stayed late for the past few nights, Mrs. Findley took off after Sandy announced she was feeling better.

The meal, scrounged from the refrigerator and pantry, was fun and filling. Once again, Sam had to acknowledge that things were going better simply because Lynn was there.

"Anybody want more fruit salad?" Lynn asked, holding up the big plastic bowl. "Going once, going twice..."

"Me!" Allie raised her hand and waved it in the air. "I want some more." She was wearing an attractive outfit of dark green pants and a multicolored sweater. The new clothes were temporarily protected by an apron, which made her look older and more domestic. Her hair was freshly shampooed and held back neatly by barrettes. She looked like a teenager. But she was acting like Allie.

Like a happy, well-adjusted kid.

"I want some, too," Sandy chimed in. "There's enough for everyone," Lynn said. She served them each another helping and the girls dug in, exclaiming how good it was.

After eating, Lynn and Allie cleared the dishes while Sam washed up and loaded the dishwasher. Sandy went off to get dressed. No one delegated the jobs, no one commented or complained.

And when Sandy emerged from the bedroom, she looked perfect. The outfit was a pearly gray that made her peaches-and-cream complexion glow and her hair shine with highlights.

"One of your new dresses?" Sam asked.

"Yeah." Sandy smoothed the velvet material of the dress. "Beverly and Lynn helped me choose it. Like it, Daddy?"

"I do, honey." Sam went over and hugged her. "You look like a million dollars tonight. I'm really glad you're feeling better."

"Me, too." Sandy hugged him back.

Sam glanced at Lynn when he thought she wasn't looking. He even allowed her to apply a little cover-up makeup to his daughter's face. It was for a performance, after all.

The concert was held at a small theater hall and, judging from the cars and the crowd waiting to go inside, it was going to be well attended. Sam explained that musicians and music lovers from all around the city and even the region would come to hear Whitney Bailey's special students perform.

"It's not only entertaining for them, but a number of scouts for well-established music programs come and check out the students."

"I though all Whit's students were special."

"They are." Sam turned toward her and lowered his voice. "But some have that extra quality that the professionals recognize. Sandy, according to those who know, has it. That's why she was offered the chance to go to Chicago."

Before Lynn could comment, Sandy nudged her father. "Daddy, we have to take the cello in through the back door."

"We can go on around front," Allie said to Lynn. "We have reserved seats."

Lynn agreed, and they walked side by side through the parking lot. After they had gone a little way, Allie reached over and took Lynn's hand.

"I'm sure glad you're here," she said. "Daddy's so much happier tonight."

"It doesn't have much to do with me. I think he's just happy with you two," Lynn replied, not ready to take credit for Sam's mood. "I think it really got to him when you misbehaved in school."

"I'd do it again, if the same thing happened," Allie announced grimly. "I hate being called a liar more than anything!"

Lynn squeezed her hand. "I understand."

"That's the really neat thing about you," Allie said. "You do understand me and Sandy. What we feel. Most grown-ups don't."

Lynn didn't answer. She did understand the frustration of having a dream and being blocked by other "grown-ups."

The doors opened, and they followed the crowd inside.

Their seats were in the center, near the front, and Allie found them immediately. "I guess you do this pretty often," Lynn said as they sat. "I mean the concert. Listening to your sister."

"Um-hmm." Allie slouched in her seat. "Sometimes it gets pretty boring."

Lynn laughed. "Well, I guess so. But look, you get to dress up and all these people get to see you. My family sometimes comes to watch me race, but I don't think it's just because I'm there. I think they like it, too."

Allie sat back up. "Can I watch you race sometime?"

"I'd like that."

"When?"

Lynn caught a glimpse of Sam making his way down the aisle. "Soon, I hope," she said. "Very soon."

Sam took the seat beside her. "Sandy's very tense," he said, his tone worried. "I hope she really isn't sick."

"Just stage fright," Lynn replied. "She told me so."

Sam's eyebrows rose. "Oh?" His voice held an odd tone, but she had no time to follow up with a question. The curtain rose, the musicians filed on stage and the concert began.

Sam explained that during the first part of the program, Sandy would play with the orchestra, but during the second half, she would move forward to play a solo. Lynn detected pride in Sam's whispered tone.

Lynn sat spellbound. Classical music wasn't exactly her all-time favorite, even when her mother had been active in the symphony programs, but tonight, she had to admit, she was liable to become a fan.

Maybe it was Sandy Russell's unbelievable genius. The sweet, sweeping sounds the child coaxed from her cello actually brought tears to Lynn's eyes more than once.

Maybe it was that.

But maybe it was Sam's hand covering hers, enfolding hers, squeezing hers as the program progressed. Maybe it was the amazing affinity she felt with him in his obvious love for his child and pleasure in her achievement and talent.

Maybe it was that.

Maybe it was just that she liked having Sam Russell close and holding her hand.

Intermission came far too soon. Sam released her hand and turned toward her. "Well," he said. "That's what she can do. What do you think about her now?"

"I'm kind of at a loss for words to describe my feelings," Lynn admitted. "I had no idea."

Sam smiled.

They went out into the lobby during intermission and had lemonade and cookies that had been prepared by some parents of the performers. Sam explained that there was a parents' group that did things to enhance the programs for the attendees as well as the children. "I'm less involved than I ought to be," he confessed. "But time—"

"Why, there you are, Sam Russell!" An elegantly dressed and coiffured woman about forty years of age came up to Sam's side and took his arm familiarly. "So good to see you again! My, the children are playing divinely, and they all look so darling this evening, especially your Alexandra. That is the loveliest dress she has on. Wherever did you find it? Hello, Allison. Don't you look sweet in that outfit. Sam, you must share your shopping secret with me. I don't think I've ever seen your children look so...nicely groomed."

Lynn saw Sam take a breath to speak. He didn't make it.

"I do believe we have a talent agent here tonight from New York," the woman continued. She held on to Sam still, but also extended her hand toward Lynn. "And who might this charming woman be?"

"I'm—" Lynn began, grasping the beringed, long-nailed, limp hand.

"So glad you all are here!" the other gushed without waiting to hear Lynn's name. She drew back her hand and held Sam with both hands. "She's a doll, Sam. I do congratulate you on keeping such gracious company, sweetie. Now, I must keep moving." She stood on tiptoe, kissed Sam's cheek and whirled away.

"Whew," Lynn said. "That happen often?"

Sam's smile was wry. "Mrs. Clyde is a bit of a so-shark, isn't she? As to how often she latches on to me like that—every time I come to a concert, I'm afraid. I'm one of the few eligible unmarrieds in this bunch. That makes me a prime target for every matron who fancies herself a matchmaker." He took a drink of lemonade and looked around. "Where's Allie?" he asked.

"She's over there." Lynn pointed to a group of older children. "Talking to that boy."

"Mmmm." Sam frowned.

"Anything wrong?"

"No. I just thought of something." He looked at her. "Did Mrs. Clyde think you and I were... involved?"

"Somewhere in there, I got the idea she might."

Sam smiled. "Well?" He sobered, his handsome face taking on its usual unemotional, noncommittal expression.

Lynn felt her skin tighten pleasantly, electrically. "Well, what?"

"Well, are we?" He smiled again, this time some excitement, even sexy mystery showing in his eyes.

Lynn felt strange things happen to her muscles and particularly to her knees. They went all weak and... like jelly!

She tried to reply lightly. "I don't know, Sam. Are we?"

He took a last drink of lemonade, emptying the paper cup. "I don't know," he said. "I guess we'll have to see, won't we?"

The lights went on and off, signaling the resumption of the concert. Allie left her friend and came over to rejoin them.

"That's a boy I like," she said. "He said he thinks I look great tonight," she whispered, just loud enough for Lynn to hear. "I guess I do. Thanks. I'm so glad we came!"

Her eyes were sparkling and there was a faint blush of color on her cheeks. And Lynn knew that she hadn't applied any makeup. It had been used only to cover Sandy's bruises.

"You need to thank Beverly," she whispered back. "She picked out the clothes."

"But *you* brought her to meet us."

"Got an admirer, Allie?" Sam asked as they walked back down the aisle to their seats. "Who was that boy?"

Allie shrugged. "Nobody special," she said. "Just old Clem Sears," she added.

Lynn caught Sam's eye and managed a quick wink.

And he winked back. She felt a thrill.

The feeling lasted through the rest of the concert. The second part was even better than the first. The children were now truly inspired, Lynn decided. Their playing was downright heavenly.

Then it was time for Sandy's special solo.

There was a pause in the program while the little girl took her place in front of the orchestra and settled down. She bent over her cello, deep in concentration. Then the music started.

Lynn listened, even more entranced than before. The enchantment grew and became knowledge. Suddenly, she understood what all the fuss over Sandy was about.

She *knew* that the best possible training *must* be made available for this young talent, just as it had to be made available for Lightning's talent. She felt Sam's hand on hers, and she gripped him tightly. Emotional harmony, counterpoint to the music, joined them. They held hands through the rest of the concert, letting go only when they stood to clap for the standing ovation Sam Russell's daughter received.

"Well?" Sam turned to her when the applause finally died down. "What do you think?"

"I think she ought to go to Chicago and anywhere else that will give her the training she needs." Lynn glanced at him. "I had no idea she was this good."

"Tell her. Please. She'll listen to you."

"I intend to," she replied.

They went backstage as soon as the crowd began to thin. Looking for Sandy, they found that she was talking to a group of other students. Lynn saw that her face was animated and her expression excited in a way that she had not noted before. Sandy really looked happy!

"Hello, dear ones!" Whit Bailey came over. "Have you ever heard Alexandra play so well?" he asked, grasping Sam's shoulders. "I was literally transported!"

"She was good tonight," Sam replied.

"Good! She was inspired!" Whit turned to Lynn. "And I understand I have you to thank, Lynn."

"Me?"

"Alexandra confessed that she was not coming tonight until you spoke to her. Made her see why she felt badly. Encouraged her." Whit held Lynn's hand in both of his. "I cannot tell you how grateful I am."

"I just... talked to her, Professor. I didn't do anything special."

Whit Bailey pulled her in and kissed her cheek. "How wrong you are, my dear. You did do something special and you are very special yourself to have reached the heart of that child." He regarded her and said, "I owe you a great deal, young lady. Please don't forget that." He turned to Sam. "Is there anything I can do to reward this grand person?"

"Daddy! Lynn!" Sandy spotted them and came running over, interrupting any response Sam could have made to Whit Bailey. "How was I?"

"Terrific, honey!" Sam gathered her up in his arms and lifted her for a hug. "I don't think I've ever heard you do so well before."

Sandy said nothing, but she hugged his neck tightly.

They stayed around for a while longer, receiving congratulations. Lynn listened, mostly, not entering conversations unless she was directly addressed. It became clear to her, however, that young Sandy Russell was on her way to a fabulous destiny.

If she was guided in the right way.

Like Lightning.

Finally Sam turned to Lynn. "I guess we have to drive you home," he said, his tone jovial. "Since you have no car."

"I guess." Lynn turned around and spoke to the girls. "Want to spend the night at my place?"

"Oh! Can we, Daddy? Can we?"

"I don't know. Tomorrow is a school day."

"It's a long drive back, Sam," Lynn reminded him. "By the time you take me home and come back, it'll be well after one in the morning. Won't they be better off sleeping over and taking off early?"

He hesitated, then answered. "You may be right. Are you sure your father and Cynthia won't mind?"

"They won't. I guarantee it," Lynn said. The girls shrieked with delight.

"And," Sam said softly, "if I can, I'll take a look at your great-grandfather."

Lynn reached over and touched his hand.

The McKinney household was mostly settled down for the night when they parked in the driveway. Lynn suggested they go to the kitchen for a snack. J.T. was there, finishing off a piece of Lettie Mae's rhubarb pie. He greeted Sam and the girls warmly, added his own invitation that they spend the night out at the guest house. In reply to Sam's inquiry, J.T. said Hank was asleep. "He's feeling a little bit better,"

J.T. explained, "but he is damn cranky. I think we ought to leave him alone tonight."

Sam agreed. "Rest is the best thing for him right now," he said. "If he's on antibiotics, he'll need to let the course run before I could do anything for him, anyway."

"Still," J.T. said, "we all appreciate you being willing."

Tyler, who had wandered into the kitchen during the conversation, stood to one side, his hands in his jeans pockets. "I think Doc Purdy's set up an appointment with our family dentist for later on this week," he said. "Not that you aren't kind to offer."

Lynn felt herself stiffen at Tyler's words and tone. He sounded less than friendly.

"Of course." Sam nodded at Tyler. His tone was formal, the first time she'd heard him speak like that for a while. "You ought to stay with the practitioner who makes Mr. Travis most comfortable."

Maybe he had sensed Tyler's strangeness as well, Lynn thought. But the kids clearly hadn't.

Sandy and Allie had taken seats at the big kitchen table. "My daddy can fix anybody's teeth problems," Allie announced. "Even Mr. Travis's."

"I'm sure of that, sweetheart," J.T. said, smiling at the child. "Would you like some of this pie? I think there's a little bit left."

"Sure," the kids chorused, looking at their father briefly for permission.

"Ice cream, too?" asked Tyler, pushing away from the wall and heading for the freezer. "We have lots of that."

"How about some coffee?" Lynn said, going over to the counter. Tyler's reversion to friendly hospitality was a relief. For a moment there, she'd wondered whether her older brother didn't like Sam or the girls.

Silly thought, of course. Tyler had no reason in the world to dislike any of the Russells.

"That's sounds great." Sam was at her side. "Let me help." His body was close enough for her to feel his warmth.

"You're a guest," she said, smiling up at him.

"I'd rather be a friend," he said, his voice low enough so that only she heard. His fingers brushed her hand.

Lynn looked at him quickly, but saw nothing in his eyes that indicated he'd meant anything special. "Okay," she said. "You get the water and the filter. I'll get the coffee. We keep it in the refrigerator."

When he touched her again, it was only by accident as they moved around, preparing the food and drink. Tyler stayed and he and Sam seemed to hit it off all right, so she forgot about the earlier tension she had sensed.

LATER, LYNN ESCORTED the three Russells to the guest house, which was empty since Ruth and Tyler were away. The girls were extremely sleepy and went inside to find the bathroom and beds, so Lynn left Sam at the door. "I'll come by and wake you all up when I come back from working Lightning in the morning. That'll be early enough that you'll have plenty of time to drive home, change and get to work and school with no problems."

"That early?"

"Before the birds are up," she replied.

Sam glanced inside to see where his children were. "I'll be there to watch you," he said. "No matter how early."

"Oh, Sam. There's no need—"

"Hush." He put his finger on her lips. "You came to hear Sandy play. You've made my kids happy. The very least I can do is watch you and your horse before I meet with Phil and Dan on Friday." He kept his finger on her lips.

"Well, okay." She felt her heart start to beat faster and her skin seemed hot all of a sudden. "Want me to throw some pebbles at your window to wake you?"

"No need." He slid his finger down to tilt up her chin. He kissed her lips lightly. "I'll just be there. And let's plan on having dinner tomorrow night, if you don't have any other commitments. Sandy has no lesson, since the concert was tonight. Mrs. Findley will stay over with them. Just the two of us, this time. So we can talk. I know a nice place."

"I... All right. Of course, I'm not doing anything else. Until I met you, I—"

"Shh. No secrets yet." He traced the line of her jaw, making sweet sensations on her skin. "Soon enough, though, I hope." Another soft kiss. "Good night, Lynn."

And before she could react, he had stepped inside and closed the door.

But react, she certainly did! She wanted him. Pure and simple.

CHAPTER ELEVEN

THE NEXT MORNING, Lynn was up well before the sun. She hauled on her riding clothes, feeling the ache of fatigue in her muscles, but knowing that would disappear once she was on her horse. She went out through the kitchen door and made her way to the stables. One bright star still shone, but the sky was starting to go pewter-silver in anticipation of the dawn. A few birds were already making morning noises. But everything else was still.

Lightning heard her coming and called out. His whinny rang in the darkness, and Lynn whistled a greeting. She went into the tack room and got out her small racing saddle and Lightning's special bridle. A handful of oat treats was already in her pocket. She hefted the saddle onto her shoulder and made her way in the warm, horsey-smelling darkness to his stall. "Here I am, boy," she said. "How're you?"

Lightning *whoofed.*

"I'm tired," said Sam Russell.

Lynn yelped and turned around. "Good grief, you scared me!"

"Sorry." He moved. She could hear straw rustling under his feet, but she still couldn't see him. "I didn't know when you'd be down, so I've been waiting here a while."

She set the saddle on top of the stall door. "Sam, you didn't have to get up this morning."

"You got up. So did I. Actually, I never got to sleep. I always have trouble in a strange bed." He took the saddle in his hands. "Let me help."

Now, she saw him. The light was clearer. His face looked drawn, his eyes weary. He had a scruffy look, and she realized he hadn't shaved. But his voice was gentle and his presence made her feel . . . good.

"You can help," she said. "But keep your distance at first. He's not used to anyone else being with me this early."

"Just you and the beast." Sam chuckled. Then he said, "What if something happened? Who would know you were hurt?"

"Oh, nothing's going to happen to me." She opened the stall and went in. Lightning nuzzled her and lipped for his oat treats. She dug some out of her pocket. "I'm a very careful horse person, you know," she added.

"Good to know." He didn't sound convinced. But he assisted as she readied the horse and led him out. Once she was in the saddle, Lightning danced and sidestepped for a moment in anticipation, and she smiled, but reined him in. For now.

She rode him at a slow walk down the path to the flat racecourse she had persuaded her father to grade out for her several years before. It was a good way from the house, Sam observed as he followed on foot at a respectful distance from Lightning's hooves.

"They all know where I am every morning," she assured him. "If something happened, Hank or Lettie Mae would notice I didn't show up when I should. They're both up by now."

"Really?"

"Well, maybe not Hank if he's still feeling under the weather. But otherwise . . ."

"He's up this early? I guess he doesn't miss much."

"Exactly. And the cowboys usually are around. You might not see them right now, but they're up and working. Ranching's a twenty-four-hour, twelve-month-a-year business." They entered the track. Lynn pointed at the wooden bleachers set up to the south of the track. "Go sit over there and watch."

The quiet authority in her voice and the seriousness of her attitude intrigued him. He did what she told him to do without hesitation, settling himself on the cold, damp wooden seat, as the chill of the morning finally hit him. He shivered. He rubbed his eyes and face, trying to get some wakefulness into his tired mind. Dawn was breaking off to the east, a thin line of color staining the sky, but it was still night where they were. The landscape was a study in black and grays. A Texan chiaroscuro. He hugged himself, hunched over and watched the woman and the horse walk sedately down to the far side of the track. They became a darkish blot against the gray ground.

The pair came plodding back up the track toward him, walking slowly as before. But now, Lynn had raised herself in the stirrups so that she rode almost on top of the saddle, or so it seemed from the distance and with the light as poor as it still was. A small, trim figure atop the huge form of the animal. Sam smiled and started to wave when she passed by the bleachers.

But she wasn't aware of him. He saw that the instant her features became clear. She was no longer aware of anything but the horse. Sam settled back.

Lynn and Lightning went around the track a few more times, slowly. She was warming the animal up, Sam realized. Just like any athlete. But the very moment the sun broke over the low clouds on the horizon, she let Lightning loose.

And in that moment Sam Russell's life changed forever.

He had never been to a horse race. So nothing had prepared him for the equine thunder that roared up the track toward him. Lightning tore around the curve so fast, Sam wouldn't have been sure it actually happened if the pounding of the mighty hooves hadn't shaken the bleachers.

The horse and rider ran as one. They made the very air quiver with the energy of their race as they sped around the dirt track. Sam stood, unable to remain still. If this had been a race, no living thing could have caught them. Sam knew now that everything Lynn McKinney had promised him about Lightning's potential was true.

So true he had to become a part of it. Something inside him exploded into fireworks of excitement. All weariness faded, and he wanted to jump and holler and . . .

Tell Lynn about his growing desire for her.

Sam sat back down, his heart pounding in his chest. Lynn and Lightning made the circuit and slowed. He sat very still as they cantered back past him. She was up in the stirrups again now, and still concentrating on her mount. But he saw her glance at him. Maybe she was trying to read his thoughts. Sense his reaction.

If she only knew!

Lynn let Lightning move around the track at his own pace for a while. The morning sun was completely up by the time the horse settled into a walk. His coat was shiny with sweat, and the heat of his body steamed in the damp air. Lynn rode up to the bleachers and reined Lightning in. He huffed, but was willing to stop.

"Well," she said to Sam, "what do you think?"

The sun was on his face. "I think," he said, "that anyone who doesn't listen to you when it comes to dealing with this overgrown nag is crazy." He stood up, hands jammed into his pockets. "Frankly, Lynn, I've never seen anything like this before."

"Really?" She felt energy surging through her. Lightning sensed it and sidestepped quickly. "Really?"

"Yes." Sam got down from the bleachers. "And I intend to convey my feelings to Phil and Dan at the earliest opportunity." He came over to Lightning and regarded the animal intently. "I think it's a sin not to give this guy a chance at the big races. He was born to run."

"He was, wasn't he?" Lynn wanted to jump off and grab Sam, but she kept her seat. "Oh, you don't know how much hearing you say that means to me."

Sam reached out and gingerly touched the horse's nose. Lightning tolerated it. "Don't tell me right now, okay? We can discuss it after my meeting on Friday," he said. "I'd rather keep the time between us this evening on a social level. No business. Is six o'clock all right for you tonight?"

"I'll be ready."

BY THE TIME Lynn had cooled Lightning down and turned him back into his stall, she was anxious to see the three Russells again and pick up where they had left off. She didn't even go upstairs to change out of her riding gear before she went into the kitchen.

Lettie Mae and Virginia were the only ones there. "Where's Sam?" Lynn asked. "Hasn't he come in yet?"

"Come and gone, child," Lettie Mae responded, handing her a mug of coffee. "Come and gone. He scooped up those girls of his so fast they didn't have time to even finish eating."

"Oh." Lynn sat down at the table.

"Honey, is there something serious going on between you and that man?" Virginia's tone was kind. "First he comes in here, gets his kids and hurries out. Odd expression on his face, let me tell you. Even the children seemed to think their daddy was acting strange. And now here you are, looking like you just lost your best friend."

Lynn sipped coffee. It was hot as fire and full of rich flavor. It did nothing to relieve the foolish feeling of disappointment at finding Sam already gone. "I thought..." she began. "I don't know."

"Hmm," said Lettie Mae. She and Virginia looked at each other.

"Maybe you ought to take a little nap," suggested the housekeeper, offering one of her standard suggestions for emotional ills. "Rest your mind. Then maybe you can see a bit clearer how things really are."

"Maybe." Lynn drank more coffee. "But I'm not sure it'll help. I'm not sure at all."

"Mmm," the two older women both said. Then they looked at each other again and nodded solemnly.

Lynn grinned, but didn't give them the satisfaction of rising to the bait. She still wasn't exactly sure that she knew what was on the hook!

While Lynn was dealing with her strange feelings, Sam encountered yet another change he could attribute to her. Once they arrived home, the girls showered quickly and changed into new school clothes, did their chores and helped him prepare breakfast without a gripe or fuss. While they were eating, it happened.

"I think I might want to go to Chicago," Sandy announced without any preamble.

Sam stopped himself from spitting out coffee. "Oh? Really?"

"Yeah." She munched on her food. "Beverly says it's a pretty neat city. She's been there lots, and she and Lynn promised that they would both come visit me, if I went." She drank orange juice. "Besides, I look okay now. Everybody says so. In these clothes, nobody will make fun of me 'cause I come from Texas.''

Sam tried to make sense of that, but it was way beyond him. "What's wrong with being from Texas?" he asked, mystified.

Sandy made a face. "When we visited up there some girl told me I talked funny."

"Oh. Well, you have different accents. Didn't she sound funny to you?"

"Yeah. But she was from there. That makes it okay."

"See, Daddy," Allie interjected, "if Sandy looks good like this, and if Lynn and Beverly came to see her, nobody'd make fun. They'd be too impressed."

"Oh."

"So, anyway, I think I might go." Sandy returned her attention to her breakfast.

"And I think she should," Allie said in a voice that indicated case closed. "Maybe," she added quietly, almost to herself, "I'll try again for Space Camp. But I have to think about it."

"That's fine, honey. That's what you should do. Make up your own mind." And Sam Russell drank his coffee, marveling at the complexity of the females in his life, and wondering whether he would ever understand them.

THAT EVENING, Lynn stood before her mirror, trying on some gold jewelry Cynthia offered to lend her. Beverly had dropped by, and she, as well as Cynthia, hung around to make comments and suggestions as well as tease Lynn about her new beau. Lynn took the kidding in good spirit, but felt it was getting a bit too close to the truth for comfort.

"We're just going out to dinner," she said, trying not to let her feelings show. "It's not a big deal, and I wish you all wouldn't act like it is."

"He did send you more flowers," Cynthia pointed out. Another large bouquet of roses had arrived late that morning. "He really appreciates you, Lynn."

"Why, he's just a real gentleman," Beverly said. "Kind and considerate. Lynn, you look gorgeous."

"Thanks." Lynn regarded her reflection. She did look pretty good, actually. The navy-blue dress was flattering, no denying it. "I kind of expected him to stay ballistic over our spending all that money on the girls' clothes. Not for him to be grateful to us."

"Don't be silly. Any daddy likes to see his girls looking nice." Beverly tucked a stray golden curl back into her own hairdo. "I know mine always did," she added.

Lynn patted her cousin's arm. Beverly was finally coming out of grieving over her father, but her voice still broke whenever she mentioned him.

"How was Hank feeling today?" Lynn asked Cynthia, to change the topic. "He was sitting out on the porch this afternoon, and he seemed okay when I spoke with him. Quiet, but okay."

"He's much better."

"Is he going to Dr. Sam for that awful tooth thing?" Beverly asked.

"We don't know yet," Cynthia said quickly. "He may. It depends."

On what Tyler finds out about Sam Russell, Cynthia thought.

SAM PULLED off the highway onto the Double C Ranch road right on the dot of six. Another five minutes, and he was parked in front of the house. As he climbed the steps to the porch and the big front door, he saw Hank Travis slouched in a rocking chair a few feet away, watching him. The old man's expression was less than warm.

"Evening, Mr. Travis," Sam said.

"Come for Lynnie?" Hank didn't seem at all happy at the prospect.

"Well, I'm taking her out to dinner, sir."

"You be careful with her, boy." Hank glared, then looked away into the distance. "She's a truly precious person."

"Yes, sir. I know that."

"Just be careful."

"I intend to be." He stepped closer. "How are you feeling, sir?"

"Got me a toothache." Hank clamped his lips shut.

"So I heard. Well, then, let me—"

"Nope. Don't want nobody touchin' me. Stay clear, boy."

Sam moved closer. "Come on, now. You know I'm a dentist. I'm not going to hurt you. I just—"

"Evening, Sam." The front door opened, and Tyler came out onto the porch. "Lynn's about ready. Be down in a second."

"Hi, Sam." Lynn appeared at the door. "Sorry to be late." She opened the screen and came out. She looked at him and smiled.

Sam didn't speak immediately. He couldn't. He just stared. The way her auburn hair had been arranged in soft waves around her face gave her a fresh, unexpected beauty that took his breath away.

"Sam?" Lynn moved closer. "What's the matter?"

Hank grinned and spoke carefully, with regard for his aching jaw. "Ain't nothin' wrong with him, girl. You git on, now, the two of you." He cocked his head. "Tyler, fetch me some whiskey."

"Nate said no drinking as long as you're on the antibiotics, Grandpa, and you know it good and well."

"Hell of a thing," Hank said softly. But to Lynn's amazement, he didn't argue. He just stared off into the distance. Then he struggled to his feet. "All right, have it your way. Think I'll lie down a spell before supper, anyways. Damn medicine's makin' me sleepy." He took a shuffling step and leaned against the wall.

Tyler hurried to help. Lynn tried, too, but Tyler said, "You all go on. I'll see to him."

"But..." Lynn stepped back, and Sam touched her arm.

"Right now he needs to rest," Sam said softly. "Let Tyler take him inside." His fingers moved on her, almost caressing her through the sleeve of her jacket.

"Well..." She eased back against Sam, feeling the security of his body behind her. "Grandpa, are you sure?"

"Yeah. Git. Git out of here and have yourself some fun, young'n."

"Really." Tyler had his arm around Hank. He opened the front door. "Go on. See you later."

As they drove away, Sam put his hand on hers. "I know it's hard for you to see him like that. You really do love that old man, don't you."

"Yes." Lynn swallowed hard. "Most of the time I'm sure he's going to live forever. And when he gets weak or hurts too much, it just..."

"Tears you in two." He removed his hand. "I know."

They drove on for a few minutes in silence.

Then Lynn asked how the girls were doing at school.

"They're doing fine. And as far as the school is concerned the fighting incident is over. At home, we're still doing some negotiation. Call me old-fashioned, but I just can't let them think I'll tolerate that kind of behavior." Sam's tone was rueful. "I have to admit the kids did have some justification but I want them to understand that hitting out is not the best way to deal with a problem."

"That's not always easy for kids."

"I know. I guess in trying to be the only parent, I've been more strict than I need." He paused, touched her hand again. "But the girls are happy. And that means far more to me than anything else." He cleared his throat. "Sandy even said she might think about Chicago, if she could wear her new clothes there. You know, I never considered that her reluctance might be due to some self-image problem, rather than simply being nervous about leaving me and Allie."

"And now you think so?"

His hand moved back to hers. "Now, I think the three of us Russells are incredibly lucky that I was talked into investing in a racehorse a few months ago.

And that his rider is one of the most wonderful women on the planet.''

Lynn blushed. "But I didn't... Beverly did..."

"You brought your cousin to them, didn't you? You let them into your family the other night, didn't you?"

"Sam, I just did what seemed the—"

"Seemed the best thing to do?" He slowed the car. "Lynn, I'll be honest. You scare me right down to my toes."

"What?"

"I find it so very easy to... like you." He glanced at her. "That scares me. What do you think about that?"

"I find it easy to like you, too," she replied. "But it doesn't scare me to do that."

"And what would scare you?" He slowed some more. Cars started passing them. "Loving me?"

The words astonished her, but she realized the idea was not that farfetched. "I... I haven't known you long enough for that," she said, anyway.

"Nor I, you." He eased back up to speed. "But that hasn't made one damn bit of difference in how I feel."

She took a deep breath. "Sam, how smart is this for us to do?"

"Not smart at all." He laughed. "But has that ever stopped any... any lovers in the past that you know about?"

"Lovers." Lynn let the word slide over her tongue. "I don't think we're..."

"Not yet." He glanced at her again, and his eyes held heat and promise. "But we are going to be."

Lynn stared at him. If any other man had ever said those words to her in that confident a tone, after such a short friendship with her, she would set him straight instantly with her caustic reply.

But this was Sam. Not any other man.

He took her to dinner at a small restaurant. Tucked away off the road under sheltering trees, it reminded her of his house. Cozy, but elegant. Dark wood paneling on the walls, candles on the tables and waiters who were almost invisible while providing excellent service. It was a place made for romance. A place where fantasies became realities. A place where people could fall in love.

Just before they finished their coffee, rain began to fall, adding to the atmosphere of comfort and romantic anticipation.

Sam looked out the window. "Rain," he said. He looked back at her.

"Springtime," she replied, finding it hard to get her breath.

"When a man's fancy. . ." His hand covered hers, and she sensed the need in him.

"Sam."

"What?"

"I need to know what changed your mind about me."

His fingertips caressed her skin. "When I saw you ride this morning, it all came together for me."

"I guess I don't understand. Why did seeing me ride do it?"

"Listen to me." His grip tightened on her hand. "Does it really make any difference how it happened? I feel what I feel. Now. This moment. Logic has nothing to do with it. You should know that."

"I. . . I should?"

He lifted her hand and kissed her palm. A thrill went through her. "Yes," he said, gazing directly into her eyes. "You should."

Lynn worked on an answer, wondering how much she should tell him about her lack of real romantic experience. Then his gaze hit her and she knew she'd never say a word to break the spell he was weaving around the two of them. *No, Sam, I don't know. No one has ever held my hand like this or looked into my heart like this, or . . .*

"Was everything satisfactory?"

The waiter's voice made her jump. Lynn pulled her hand away, embarrassment flaming her face. Of course, no one else could know what she was thinking. But she blushed anyway. Her gaze fell to the tablecloth.

Sam spoke. "It was. Please tell Bert how much I appreciated the special attention. The meal was excellent." He handed over a credit card.

"Thank you, Dr. Russell." The waiter departed.

Sam regarded Lynn. He rested his chin on his hand, one finger partly covering his mouth. "I see I've made you uncomfortable," he said. "Of course. I'm too eager. And I'm moving too fast. I—"

"Too fast?" She found herself laughing. "Too fast? For a woman who races horses? I don't think so, Sam. It's just that I've never..."

"Never what?" He looked puzzled.

She blushed again and looked away.

He was quiet for a moment. Then, "Lynn," he said softly, "I'm a fool not to have seen it sooner. It's what your great-grandfather was trying to tell me. Lynn, are you..."

The waiter returned, interrupting whatever Sam had been going to say. Sam wordlessly signed the slip and replaced the plastic card in his wallet. The waiter disappeared again, and Sam got to his feet. "Let's go," he said. His manner was brisk.

They were in the privacy of the car before he spoke again. And when he did, his words astonished her.

"I'm an absolute fool when it comes to women. I have no idea from one minute to the next what's going on with you. *Any* of you! Grown-up kinds or kids." He gripped the steering wheel with both hands.

"That's because you had no sisters, Sam. No basic training."

"And you have brothers, so you understand men?" His hands rested on the wheel, relaxing a little. He hesitated, then added gently, "And that's why you've never taken one to bed? Because you know us too well?"

A laugh burst out of her. "I guess that's right," she said. "You aren't all that much of a mystery to me, so none of you have exactly rung my bells." She hesitated. "Until now." She turned her face toward him. "Until now, Sam."

"Oh, damn." He took his hands from the wheel and put them on her face, holding her gently, as if she were a precious work of art. "Lynn, I want to make love to you so much I ache. But I will not until we..."

"Until we what, Sam?" She moved closer and slid her arms around his waist, feeling the warmth and lean strength of his body. "Until we wait until we're sure about this thing between us?"

"I..."

"Sam, I'm twenty-five. I've never had a lover. I've never wanted a man before like I want you."

He looked at her, his gaze probing deep into her eyes, seeking her heart. "You make it very difficult for me to do the right thing, Lynn." His fingers traced the line of her cheek and jaw, sending sensual shivers all through her. "Very difficult," he said, his voice getting thick and husky.

Lynn leaned back.

Sam kissed her.

CHAPTER TWELVE

IT WAS PAST FOUR in the morning when Sam dropped Lynn back at the ranch. They had spent the time in Sam's kitchen, drinking coffee and talking. Both had agreed that it was too soon to make love—they still had a lot to learn about each other. And, of course, they still had the business with Lightning to deal with. "I want you to make a rational decision about the investment. I don't want our relationship to get in the way," Lynn had told Sam. And he had agreed.

Once home, Lynn thought she'd made it in without being noticed. She used the back stairs and tossed off her good clothes, dragging on jeans and boots. She hurried outside where the day would soon dawn and worked Lightning on the long lead for longer than usual so the animal wouldn't be neglected. He seemed content when she groomed him with special care and gave him an extra helping of oat treat. She whispered a few secrets to him, then headed back to the house for breakfast.

Her entire family, minus Cal, was in the kitchen, obviously waiting for her. She greeted them, got coffee and sat down.

Hank spoke first. "Well, missy. What do you have to say for yourself?"

"Grandpa," J.T. said. "Let her get some coffee in her, first. Then she can tell us what—"

"J.T.," Cynthia said, "I told you not to—"

"Where the hell were you all night?" Tyler asked, his voice tight and his face censorious.

Lynn stared. "What?"

"I said, where were you?" Tyler stood up and began to pace. "You didn't come home last night."

Lynn looked around. Virginia, Lettie Mae, her father and her great-grandfather all seemed to approve of Tyler's tactics. Only Ruth and Cynthia were sympathetic. Ruth was clearly trying not to interfere, however, and Cynthia was obviously more concerned with J.T.'s blood pressure than Lynn's dilemma.

"I came home," she said. "When I did it is my business." She sipped her coffee. "Anyone here have a problem with that?"

There was silence for a moment. From the feel of the atmosphere, she could tell almost everyone did.

"I do." Tyler sat back down. He rubbed his face with his hand. "But you're right, Lynn. No matter how I feel about it, I guess I'm out of line. You are a grown woman."

"That's right," Ruth said quietly. She put her hand on Tyler's shoulder. "If she was your brother, you wouldn't have such a fit about it, would you? In fact, you not only wouldn't say a word, you wouldn't think a thing of it."

Lynn waited, sending Ruth a look of gratitude.

"No, I wouldn't." Tyler looked at the table. "But she's not a man, and she's my little sister. I don't want her hurt."

"Give her hell, son. Don't back down!" Hank slapped his hand on the table. "You gonna have young'ns of your own someday, Tyler, boy, and you can't let 'em—"

"Lynn's not Tyler's child," J.T. said. "She's mine." He sighed. "I just have to say we were all worried about you, honey. Wish you'd called."

Lynn looked at her father guiltily. "I should have. I'm sorry about that. We were at his house, but time just got away."

"I told him to take care with you, damn it all," Hank fumed. "Keepin' you out all night ain't no way of doin' that. And so tell me, when's he gonna marry—"

"Hank!" Cynthia cut in. "That's enough."

Lynn stood up. "I guess I shouldn't be so surprised at the way some of you are acting about this, but I am disappointed. After all, like Ruth said, not one of you ever raised a word about Cal or Tyler when they had...overnight romances. Now, just because I'm a woman, the roof's falling in. I thought this family was more understanding and sensible than this.'' She set down her coffee mug and left the room.

Behind her, she heard voices raised in comment and argument. Ruth called her name. But she didn't want to hear. She went upstairs and lay down on her bed to rest for a while. She felt good and bad.

When's he gonna marry...

Hank's question rolled around in her mind. It was one that hadn't occurred to her before. If Hank hadn't said the word...

Marriage. To Sam?

Well, didn't she love him? She thought she did. Was she lying to herself?

No.

The girls? If she married Sam, she'd be a step-mother. Something she'd sworn she'd never be. But it wasn't her fault she'd fallen for their daddy, was it? It wasn't wrong, was it?

Marriage? Out of the question. She was too young. She had too many things to do. She couldn't be married, raise two almost teenage girls and race Lightning.

Out of the question! It was definitely out of the question.

But she kind of liked the idea.

No, it was too soon, and she was being silly even to think about it.

Besides, Sam hadn't asked her. Yet.

SAM GOT BACK to his house before the girls or Mrs. Findley woke. He undressed quickly and took a shower, thinking about Lynn and himself all the while. He was standing in front of the sink, wrapped in a towel, shaving, when he heard stirrings.

"Hey, Daddy." Allie stuck her head in the door. "Have fun last night?"

"Um." Sam rinsed off his razor. He stared at his reflection. A thought was forming slowly in his mind.

"Daddy?"

"Oh, yeah."

"Daddy, when's she coming here again?" Allie had opened the door and was standing there, regarding him with an odd expression on her face. Sandy was behind her, listening. Her expression was a mirror of her sister's.

"I don't know, honey," he said, wiping his face clean. "We didn't make any plans..." He was about to say "yet," but the words trailed off around another idea that had bloomed in his brain like a small, healthy rosebud....

Marriage... To Lynn...

Allie turned around and spoke to Sandy. "I was afraid of this," she said. "He's doing it again."

Sandy nodded, then tears filled her eyes. She sniffed and ran away down the hall. Sam heard her burst into crying and heard Mrs. Findley asking what was the matter.

"Hey!" he said, taking his robe off the hook and shrugging into it. "What'd I say? Why's she crying? Allie?" he asked, belting the robe.

The older girl glared at him. "You had one date. That's it. Now we won't see her again. Like always."

"What?"

"You do it all the time, Daddy. You get to know a lady. You ask her out. Maybe we like her, maybe we don't, but we never see her after that."

"I do?" Sam was genuinely puzzled. "I do that?"

"Yes, you do." Allie turned and headed down the hall for the kitchen.

"I guess I do." Speaking to himself, Sam stood alone in the bathroom. He thought about it. Looked at his reflection. Thought about himself. And Lynn. And his children. Moments passed. He went out into the hall.

"I want to marry her!" he yelled. "Will that make everybody happy?" He was grinning like an idiot. The idea made him downright blissful.

Silence, then shrieks of joy. From the wildly enthusiastic response, Sam gathered it would.

AT THE RANCH more roses arrived late that morning. Sam sent five dozen of them this time. The whole house was soon fragrant with their rich perfume. Lynn received the luxuriant gift with joy in her heart. He did love her. She was sure.

And she loved him. A man who was so wonderful, sexy, thoughtful and kind and sweet couldn't help but be lovable. That was as clear to her as the crystal vases holding the roses.

It was also clear now to her family that more was going on than just a friendly relationship.

And the Sam issue hung in the air at the Double C like a strange storm cloud. Lynn found herself becoming concerned. There was more going on than just worrying about her. Something else was afoot involving Sam, she was sure. But she could not get anyone to give her an indication of what it was.

She needed to talk, and no one was talking.

THE GLOW OF HAPPINESS that filled Sam when he thought of proposing marriage to Lynn lasted until his luncheon meeting with Phil and Dan.

The moment he walked into the dining room of the private club where they had agreed to meet, and saw them, he knew there was trouble in the air. Dan's face was ruddy from drink and anger and Phil's lean visage was nearly as pale as the martini he was sipping. Sam knew the two men weren't the kind to show such deep emotion unless there was a very good reason.

Or a very bad reason, depending on your point of view.

"Siddown, you rat," Dan slurred as Sam came up to the table.

"Huh?" Sam just stood there. "What?"

"I said *sit,*" Dan snarled, kicking at the chair in front of Sam. "We gotta talk, you and us."

"Dan, you're drunk. I don't 'gotta talk' with either of you as long as you're—"

"Sam, please." Phil made a conciliatory gesture. "Sorry. We're just real upset."

Sam sat. "I can see that."

"Wanna know why?" Dan took another drink of his whiskey. "Or can you tell us?"

"Dan, shut up." Phil reached down into his briefcase and took out a thick folder. "I don't think he knows. He wouldn't have come, if he did."

"Maybe." Dan's concession sounded grudging. "Maybe he's just doin' this to throw us off the track."

"What's going on?" Sam ignored Dan and spoke to Phil.

"All things in good time, my boy," Phil said. He opened the folder. "You know the little bitch that's giving us so much trouble over that damn race-horse?"

"Lynn? Sure, I—"

"Oh, *Lynn*, is it?" Dan leaned forward, spilling some of his drink. "Isn't that just cozy as hell?"

"I mean you *know* her?" Phil was grinning, a leering expression. "Like biblically?"

Sam sat back and put his hand up to his face, partially masking his mouth. "None of your damn business, Phil."

Dan laughed, an ugly sound.

"Oh, I think it is," Phil continued, handing over a thick sheaf of computer printout. "Take a look for yourself."

Sam did. Curiosity was driving him as much as anger at the two men and their nasty insinuations. He examined the pages for a moment.

"What the hell?" He leaned over the table, his hand on the printout and his eyes on Phil. "Where did you get this?"

"Connections," Phil said. "Just be glad I have 'em."

"Is this verified?"

"Sure as hell is." Dan slammed his hand down on the table. "I paid a little call on the old broad who's doing the investigation and leaned on her some."

"And?" Sam turned to the other man.

Dan shrugged and lost some of his tough-guy look. "Well, she didn't exactly fold like a rose. She's an ex-cop. But she did confirm she'd been hired to look into our business dealings because of *you.*"

"I don't believe it."

"Believe, my foolish friend." Phil tossed out a manila envelope. "Go ahead. Look," he urged.

Sam opened the envelope. There were about a dozen black-and-white pictures of him. And Lynn. At the restaurant. Embracing and kissing in his car. He cleared his throat. "Are there more?"

"No." Phil gathered up the photos and sifted them back into the envelope. "She said she wasn't doing any kind of sex investigation. Just financial and character." He paused and looked at Sam. "*Your* character, my friend."

Sam swore. His gut twisted. "Who did it?"

"Oh, come on, Doctor!" Dan reached over and shook Sam's shoulder. "The almighty McKinneys, of course. To see if you're worthy to bed their little—"

Dan didn't get any more out. Sam's fist moved and smashed into the man's face. Dan fell backward out of his chair and Sam was up and over him in a flash. The maître d' and several waiters hurried over, but Phil defused the situation.

"Oh, for God's sake," he said calmly. "Boys, boys. *We* are not the enemy."

Sam fought rage, but he stepped back. "You're right." He held out his hand to Dan. "I'm sorry. Lost my head there." He helped the other man to his feet.

Dan wiped his bleeding nose. "It's all right. I was outa line, too."

They sat back down, and the waiters faded away. Sam took a deep breath. "What can I do? It *is* my fault you've been subjected to this."

Phil smiled. "Hoped you'd take that tack, Sam. You see, the real problem isn't that old J.T. sicced his hounds on you. The real problem is our little lady jockey." He held up a hand. "No offense meant, believe me."

Sam settled. "All right. Go on. Please."

"She's putting the eggs into one basket, with no guarantees," Dan complained. "Not letting that nag run."

"She says—" Sam started to defend Lynn.

"She *says* the horse is a Triple Crown winner," Phil said, sneering. "She's dreaming."

"Really? Are you sure?"

"I can't afford to take the chance," Phil said. "Neither can Dan, and neither can you. We need income now, or we're sunk on this investment."

Sam looked at Dan. The other man nodded, sobered by the fist in his face and the facts on the table. "You two are overextended on your new building, aren't you?" Sam asked. "You found out it was a mistake for you to invest in Lightning. Got yourselves in a hole."

"Well, I wouldn't put it that way," Phil hedged.

"Yes. Hell, yes." Dan held out his hands, palms up, pleading. "Listen, Sam, we're desperate. You've got to sweet-talk her into—"

"Into what? Racing the way you want?"

"Yes." Phil set down another folder. He took out a sheet of paper and handed it to Sam. "Check this out."

Sam did. If Lynn raced Lightning the way Phil and Dan wanted, they stood to make big bucks almost immediately. Not the millions Lynn anticipated if they waited, but a nice, tidy profit. "But what about this one?" he asked, pointing to a line of print. He was sure Lynn had warned him about that kind of race, saying she'd see Lightning let loose on the range before she ran him in one like it. "Isn't it—"

"It's one where the winner's up for sale at a top price," Phil said. "By the time the horse hits that one, he'll be worth at least a hundred thou apiece for us, easy. Probably more."

"But...but then he'll be sold to someone outside our investment group. Sold so none of us, Lynn included, will own any part of him anymore."

"That's the whole idea. Quick, major profit."

Sam sat back. "I see." He tapped the paper with a finger. "And you guys want me to get Lynn to agree to this, knowing she's got her own money and more in Lightning?"

"Sure. You don't owe the bitch a thing, Sam," Dan said.

"How do you figure that?"

Dan shrugged. "The P.I. thing. Invasion of your privacy. It's insulting, if you ask me. Like some animal, having your bloodlines checked before you get to—"

"Dan, shut up," Phil said smoothly. "But he's right, Sam. These people don't think you're good enough for their little girl. For all you know, she's in on it, too. If you're smart..."

Sam stood up. "Let me think about this," he said. "I don't know quite what to think or do right now. I need some time."

"Time is one thing we haven't got a lot of," Phil said. "Dan's right. We both need the money. As soon as possible. We're doing something right now. Soon as we leave here. We're seeing a lawyer. A good one with some creativity when it comes to the law, and he's got some ideas how we can deal with the situation immediately.''

Sam took out his pocket notebook and wrote a figure on a piece of paper. He tore the sheet out of the notebook and handed it to Phil. ''Would this much take care of your problems?''

Phil looked. He nodded and shrugged. ''It would help. When would we get it?''

''I can't say yet.'' Sam returned the notebook to his pocket. ''I have some property in New Orleans I could try to sell. It'll take time, but it's better than nothing. Which is what you'll get if you try pressuring Lynn McKinney. I do know her well enough to tell you that even I couldn't budge her from her stand about that horse if my life depended on it. Think the offer over,'' he added. Then he turned and left the restaurant.

He was in no mood for lunch.

Phil and Dan watched as he walked out the door. ''You trust him?'' Dan asked. ''Will he really buy us out?''

''Hell, no.'' Phil stared glumly at the folders on the table. ''He's blowing smoke. That's all. He's too damn tied up in the girl. He'll ruin us just because of that, no matter what he promises now.''

''Then we gotta act on our own. Do something! Forget him.''

"Right." Phil straightened. He signaled the waiter. "Coffee, please." he said. "Strong, black and for both of us."

The waiter complied.

"MR. MCKINNEY, we need to talk."

Tyler felt a chill as he listened to the private investigator's voice over the phone. Effie Morris had said she would call early next week with her report. This was only Friday afternoon. And the woman sounded upset. "What's up?" he asked.

"Well, I'd rather speak to you in person, if you don't mind," Effie said. "I have doubts about the integrity of my phone line."

"What?"

"I'd rather not go into—"

"I understand," Tyler interrupted. "I can be there in, say, two hours. Will that suit?"

"Yes, it will." Pause. "Mr. McKinney, don't tell anyone where you're going."

The chill developed quickly into an icy coldness in Tyler's brain. If he read the tone right, Effie Morris had discovered something truly dreadful about Sam Russell. *Damn!* Deep down, Tyler had been praying the man would come up clean. Lynn was so in love she might as well be carrying around a sign stating the fact.

Damn!

"Okay," he agreed. "I won't."

"Good." Effie hung up.

Tyler sighed. This was not good. He went into the hall.

"Hi, there, big brother," Lynn said, calling out to him from the kitchen. "On your way out to the vines?"

"I was, but I have to go into Austin right away."

Lynn frowned. "Is there a problem?"

"What? No. Why?"

"You look kind of funny." She took a step forward. "It's not about Grandpa, is it? When I saw him, he was feeling much better."

"He still is." Tyler made himself smile and laugh. "No, this is nothing to do with family," he lied. "Just some personal stuff I have to attend to." He took his hat from the rack. "If you see Ruth, tell her I'll get back as soon as I can, all right?"

"All right." Lynn watched her older brother as he smiled again and hurried out the front door. Something was wrong. Something was wrong, and she was being shut out of it.

And if she was being shut out, it was because they were all trying to protect her.

Therefore, it must have something to do with Sam!

She turned back to the kitchen, took her cup to the sink, rinsed it out and set it on the counter. Maybe she ought not to push it, but she was darn tired of waiting for someone who knew what was going on to tell her.

She made a decision. Then she headed out into the hall. "Daddy," she yelled. "Where are you? I need to talk to you!"

SAM SAT IN HIS CAR for a long time, thinking. There was a lot going on here, and he wasn't sure he'd been told the truth yet by anyone. He had a number of options, including losing his temper at everyone involved.

But he was not going to do that. His feelings for Lynn were too important to him to risk losing her just because he couldn't control his anger. Now was a time for thoughtful behavior, not impulse.

He believed Phil. Up to a point. The McKinneys were investigating him. Sam rubbed a hand over his face and stared out the window at the passing traffic, seeing nothing. Hell, might he not do exactly the same thing if one of his own girls was seeing a guy he wasn't sure about? If there was money and deep feelings involved?

But that didn't make the insult any the less stinging. He was due for a showdown with her father over this.

And with Lynn?

Well, that depended. Did she know about the investigation? If not, she'd be madder than a wet hen!

What if she had known? Could he have misread her innocence and forthrightness completely? Was she so determined to succeed with her horse that she had entered into a conspiracy to seduce his heart, in order to...

Oh, that was insane!

But not illogical, he told himself. *Think.* It made good, cold sense. She needed him in order to get her way. Why not try to get at him through his heart?

Because that was not something Lynn McKinney would do, that's why!

Or was it? He'd known her all of a week.

He'd known her a lifetime.

Sam groaned and leaned his head against the steering wheel. Then he sat back. What had she done to his life in that one week? Anything bad?

No. Only good things had happened since he'd met her.

So she deserved the benefit of the doubt. At least until he had a chance to talk to her directly. He loved her. He had made up his mind to ask her to be his wife. Furthermore, to be the mother of his two daughters. What kind of a lover was he if the first time her integrity and love were called into question, he threw her out?

Not much of one. That was for sure. No, there were plenty of others who needed to answer some questions before Lynn did. The list formed in his mind. A list composed of the players all the way from himself to Lynn. Himself, he knew. Lynn, he was determined to trust. The last of those others was where he intended to begin to find the truth.

Sam started his car and pulled out into the traffic.

"YOU DID WHAT?" Lynn stared at her father in dismay. "You had Sam *investigated?*"

J.T. looked abashed. "Well, not exactly. You see, I told Tyler to—"

"*Tyler.*" Lynn balled her fists. "That *snake!*"

"Don't blame your brother," her father said. "He was just doing what I asked him to."

"Then it was your idea!"

"No! I didn't say that."

Cynthia rushed into the den. "What's the matter? We can hear you two all over the house."

"Daddy sent a private detective after Sam!" Lynn declared. "Oh, Cynthia, he's going to hate me! He'll believe I don't trust him."

"Lynn—" J.T. got up, moved by her passion and tears "—we can explain to him."

"What?" Lynn turned on her father. "What can you explain? That you didn't like him, so you—"

"We do like him!"

"Then why..."

"Why don't you both sit down." Cynthia motioned Lynn to a chair and took one herself. "J.T.?"

Her husband sat.

"Now, listen, Lynn. I know what your father and Tyler have done seems high-handed, but they were only acting in your best interest. They were worried about you and your future."

Lynn nodded. "But it's *my* future, Cynthia. Daddy, I love him. If he asks me, I'll marry him. I have to tell him about this. Warn him, if you want to call it that."

"You're taking his side against your own family?"

"No, Daddy." Lynn stood up. "I'm not taking sides. I am taking a stand." She went over and kissed his cheek. "I still love you, but I am really mad at you."

Then she left the room.

J.T. stared at his wife.

Cynthia was smiling faintly. "When we have a child, if he or she has half that much integrity and strength of character," she said finally, "I will be eternally delighted."

"She's stubborn! She's not strong, she's just damn stubborn!"

"Gosh, I cannot imagine where she got that trait from."

J.T. glared. Then he grudgingly grinned. "You do realize," he said, "that if Sam Russell is a bad guy, he's going to regret ever meeting my little girl."

"Oh, yes. I do realize that. You won't have to do a thing, either. Lynn will take care of him herself. She'll make him wish he'd never been born, if he betrays her. She can take care of herself, J.T. She's a grown woman with a heart and mind that just amazes me the more I get to know her. You should be very proud."

J.T. smiled, then frowned. "Actually, I am. But it sure is hard on a body, being proud of a child like that. I want to keep her safe. But I can't do that, can I?"

"No. But we can both be there if she does need us. If things don't work out."

He nodded. "Thanks. I needed to hear that. With all that's going on, I sometimes get to feeling kind of...well, kind of unneeded around here these days."

"J.T. McKinney, stop that foolish talk. Your children are finally growing up. Cut out that 'unneeded' stuff. Or, if you'd like, I'll start listing all the ways *I* need you and intend to need you for the rest of our lives."

"Hmmm." His grin was genuine and mischievous. "Start listing. I'm all ears."

CHAPTER THIRTEEN

TYLER LISTENED to Effie Morris's report with a combined feeling of relief and apprehension.

"This dentist is a decent man," the ex-policewoman told him. "He's a family man, in spite of being a young and handsome widower. He does not cat around, and I found nothing at all to indicate he was involved in any sort of shady dealing or questionable activity."

"But some of his colleagues...?"

"His partners in the racehorse investment group are not as clean. They aren't crooks, but they have some serious financial problems."

"I see." Tyler rubbed his chin. "Can you tell me more?"

"Not really. Legally, I couldn't investigate them. Just Dr. Russell. But I have a strong suspicion their investment in your sister's horse is a desperate attempt to bail themselves out of a financial hole. I do not have hard evidence, though."

"I guess that's all I need to know. Even if Sam's upright, he's tainted by association."

Effie cleared her throat. "That's not all the bad news, I'm afraid."

"What else?"

"They know about my investigation. The partners, that is."

"Oh? How?"

"I'm not sure. One of them came here yesterday and tried to intimidate me into revealing who my employer was."

"And?"

Effie smiled. It was a tight, almost wicked smirk. "Of course, I didn't tell him. But you need to be aware this has happened." Now she was serious. "Given the situation with your sister and Dr. Russell, they will probably figure out it was you who initiated the process. And I doubt if they'll keep it to themselves. They may already have told him."

"I appreciate your frankness." Tyler leaned forward and rubbed his palms together, thinking. "I guess I'd better get in touch with Sam and confess."

"No need. I know about it." Sam Russell was at the door. And he did not look happy.

MRS. FINDLEY cleared her throat and looked at Lynn. "I believe I know why you're here. Come to discuss the future." She beamed.

Lynn just looked at her, not understanding what the woman was saying. All she knew was that she had to explain things to Sam. She'd tried his office, but Tennie Williams had said he was gone for the afternoon.

"I mean, with Doctor asking you to marry him and all, I..." The housekeeper looked at Lynn's expression and broke off. She clapped her hand to her mouth. "Oh, dear. I'm telling tales out of school," she said. "He hasn't done it yet."

"I..." Lynn felt the blood drain from her face. She didn't know whether to laugh or cry. "No, he hasn't." She reached out and touched Mrs. Findley's hand. "Please, tell me why you think he's going to ask me? I swear I won't let on I know anything."

It took a little coaxing, but Mrs. Findley finally recited the events of the early morning. And Lynn had no trouble picturing the scene. Sam, standing in the bathroom, shaving. The girls upset over what they saw as the potential loss of her as a friend. And Sam...

Sam deciding on the spur of the moment to offer to marry her!

Not out of love. She felt numb. No man decides to get married because his kids are crying unless...

Unless Grandpa was right all along and he only wanted her as a legal baby-sitter!

Her heart ached. "Thanks," she said to Mrs. Findley, managing to put some feeling into the word. "I really appreciate—"

"Lynn?" The back door slammed and the girls came running down the hall into the kitchen.

"You're here!"

"We saw your car."

"I told Professor Bailey I'm going to Chicago. You and Beverly will come visit me, won't you? You promised!" Sandy was practically jumping up and down with energy and enthusiasm.

"And I might get to go to Space Camp." Allie was radiant. "The teacher gave out the applications again, and I took one." She waved some paper at Lynn. "If I go, it won't be for the whole summer, but will you and Daddy visit me anyway?"

Lynn's heart squeezed tight. How could she turn away from these two? "Sure," she said, hugging them and stroking their hair. She pulled back. "You both look very nice today."

Sandy sat at the table. "The kids at school think I'm really cool now." She accepted milk and cookies from Mrs. Findley with thanks.

Allie didn't look as happy. "My friends like my clothes, but they still think I'm lying about you and Beverly. They don't believe anything about it."

"The important thing is that you aren't lying. I bet if we asked her, Beverly'd come pick you up at school sometime and your friends could see she's real. Especially if she let you ride home in her big old Cadillac.''

"Would she? Really?''

"Wow!''

"I know she would,'' Lynn reassured them. Then she took stock of her feelings. Even if Sam didn't really love her, she loved him. And she loved these two kids.

But was it enough?

SAM GLARED at Tyler. "This makes me mad as all hell, you know,'' he said.

"I know.'' Tyler looked defensive. "But she's my sister. I won't stand by and let her get hurt. I couldn't. Dad gave me the job, and I did it. I can't help it, if you don't like it. Her well-being was our only concern, believe me.''

Sam made a conciliatory sound by way of reply. He understood those sentiments.

They had left Effie Morris's office, after a few tense moments. Now they were seated in a quiet neighborhood bar. Once beers were put in front of them, they began speaking.

"Does she know about it?'' Sam put both hands on the table, palms down.

"No.'' Tyler tried a wry smile. "And if you tell her, she'll have my liver for lunch.''

"I ought to let her."

"What you ought to do is accept my sincere apologies and forget this ever happened."

Sam tapped the table with his fingers. "If it was just me involved, I might do that. But it's gotten beyond mere forgiveness, Tyler. And I think you already know that. Because of the others involved."

"Your partners?"

"They aren't real pleased with any of this. They aren't real pleased with Lynn. Or me, for that matter." Some darker thoughts began to form in Sam's mind. "In fact, I'm concerned about the backlash. One of them mentioned something about hiring a lawyer. Lynn and I might be in for some hard days ahead over that."

Tyler looked grim. "Let 'em get a lawyer. We have one, too. A damn good one. And I know Ms. Morris violated no laws in her investigation."

"Maybe so." Sam drew lines through a ring of moisture on the tabletop. "But I don't know if that'll make a whole lot of difference. It's not just the private-eye thing with them. It's the horse."

"What can they do? They can't move without her. He's a one-jockey horse. Only Lynn can ride him."

"Maybe. They may not really believe that. Unless you've seen her on him, I don't think anyone could really understand the bond she has with that animal. I didn't until I witnessed it. I don't know what's going to happen. But I am worried."

"Then..."

"Tyler, I want to marry her. I don't want to start out by fighting with her family."

Tyler's eyebrows rose. "Marriage? Does she know this?"

Sam shook his head. "Not yet. I'm going to ask her this weekend. I love her. My kids adore her. I know we haven't known each other long, but—"

Tyler McKinney grinned. "Hey, don't try to excuse that to me. Ruth and I knew from the first moment we met that something extraordinary was going on between us. And while we took a little longer than a week to find out what it was, we were fast by any standards. So that's not the problem."

"So, what is?"

"She's my sister. That would be the problem for me with any man who got close to her so quickly and had obvious selfish motives to do so."

Sam felt his anger returning. "Damn it, Tyler, I thought I made it clear—"

"Look, Sam. Your motives are suspect, you have to admit. What do you have to lose? You need a woman for your kids. Lynn has a stranglehold on a potentially profitable investment of yours. She's young and pretty and—"

"She's beautiful!"

"Well, okay. She's my sister. Anyway, she's not wealthy, but she's not broke, either and if—"

"If the horse makes it, she'll be rich. Do you really think I've taken that into consideration?"

Tyler shrugged, not willing to comment.

Sam sat back. "We'll have many things to work out before we marry," he said. "But the way I see it, the first thing will be to ask her if she can put me and the girls before all of you."

"If you put it to her like that, you'll lose her."

"I don't think so."

The two stared at each other.

"We'll see," said Tyler.

"I guess we will," said Sam.

Both of them drank beer.

Then Tyler spoke. "Listen, Sam. I don't want this antagonism with you. I don't see it as a contest. I don't know what your family background is, but Lynn's connection to her family is special and life-long. We're not just tied to the ranch. We're deeply and permanently tied to one another, and anyone— spouse, friend or lover—who tries deliberately to cut those ties is due to lose. Everyone will lose. The pain..."

"She's a grown woman. Free to make her own choices."

"Sam, you and I are both old enough to know we're all only so free. Love binds us. If we're lucky, we welcome the ropes."

"What you're saying is that if I marry Lynn, I take on the whole family?"

"That's the deal."

Sam stared, glared, looked away. Then he started to laugh. "Well, hell, Tyler. I was an only child. Grew up in New Orleans. My folks passed away years ago, and I have no close relatives left. My kids like the lot of you. I guess I can learn to live with it, if I try real hard. I can't promise anything, though."

"Is that a declaration of a truce?"

"I think it is."

The two men grinned at each other and shook hands.

"DOES DADDY KNOW you came to see him?" Allie asked. Lynn and the girls were in the den, playing a board game. "I can't figure out why he isn't here yet. He's late."

"He doesn't know I'm here," Lynn responded. "It's a surprise."

"When you get married, he..." Allie regarded Lynn. "You are going to get married, aren't you?"

Lynn hesitated. Then she said, "I can't say yet. It depends on..."

"You don't sound too sure about it." Sam stood in the doorway. "Depends on what?"

"Daddy! You sneaked up on us!" Sandy said, running over and giving her father a hug.

"Where have you been?" Allie asked. "No one could find you. We were worried."

Lynn said nothing. She just watched him.

"I was seeing some folks," Sam said. He released Sandy. "Hello, Lynn."

"Was one of them my brother?" she asked.

"Yes."

"We need to talk."

"I know." Then Sam spoke to the girls. "I'm sorry to be so late," he said. "But I did have an important meeting this afternoon." He glanced at Lynn. "It went on a little longer than I thought it would. Now how would you kids like to go to the video store with Mrs. Findley and choose a movie. And you can order in pizza."

"Great, Daddy," Allie said. "What are you and Lynn going to do?"

Sam looked at Lynn. "Oh, we'll think of something," he said.

WITHIN TWENTY MINUTES Sam and Lynn were heading out of town in his car.

Neither of them said anything for a while.

"I love you," Lynn said finally. "No matter what has happened or will happen, you need to know."

"I know that."

"Sam, I swear I didn't know Tyler and Daddy were—"

"Honey, I know that, too. Listen, Lynn, I don't really understand the bond between you and your family, but I'm willing to learn to deal with it."

"Deal with it? That's real nice of you!"

"Hey! I'm the one who's been wronged here."

Lynn took a deep breath. "So am I."

He sighed, letting his body relax a little behind the wheel. "You're right. I was told you didn't know about the investigation. Tyler swore the investigation was his own idea."

"His and Daddy's. Some kind of protectionist conspiracy they cooked up. I didn't know until early this afternoon. Tyler left in a hurry to come into town and I've been getting some strange signals from everybody about you, so I asked a few questions."

"And got some answers, I expect." The slightest hint of laughter in his voice made her turn and look at him. He was smiling.

"You bet I did," she declared. "And when I heard them, I was furious. Why me? Why you? You can believe nobody checked on Ruth when Tyler brought her home. Or on Serena when Cal—"

"It's not the same." Sam covered her hand with his. "I don't care how much it annoys you, you are the youngest kid in your family, and female, to boot. They are just not going to let you wander off on your own without watching out after you. I tell you how I know. I would be doing exactly the same thing for my daughters."

Lynn thought about that. "I guess you're right.... Sam, pull over please."

Something in her calm but intense tone made him glance over at her. A moment later, they were pulling into a rest stop. When he parked, they both got out of the car and faced each other across the hood.

"I think we need to be totally honest with each other right now," she said.

Sam studied her carefully, a smile playing on his lips. "I don't know if total honesty is such a good idea. You wouldn't like to know everything I've been thinking."

"I'm serious, Sam. We need to talk."

Sam patted the hood with his palm. The late-afternoon sun was in his eyes, and Lynn was silhouetted against the scenery. A soft breeze was blowing, making her hair move in a slow dance around her face. He took a deep breath and plunged.

"I didn't plan to do this so abruptly and without the proper romantic touches, but I want you to marry me, Lynn," he said. "I'm not sure anything else is important."

"Why do you want to marry me?" Her arms were folded, and she sounded distant and unimpressed with his announcement.

Sam rubbed the back of his neck. "Lynn, I don't understand the question."

She came around the front of the car and he was startled to see tears in her eyes. "Maybe not. But please answer it, anyway. It's very important."

"I don't..."

She reached toward him, then let her hand drop. "Are we wrong about this? About us?"

Sam felt something inside finally fall into place. "No, we aren't wrong." He moved over and took her in his arms. She did not resist.

Nor did she embrace him.

"We aren't wrong," he said, speaking softly against her silky hair. "But it's been fast and it's been confusing and there are so many factors at work that's it's real hard to see clearly. All I know is I love you, and if I can't live with you for the rest—"

"Oh, Sam." *Now* her arms went around his neck. "You do love me! That's why you want to marry me?"

Relief flooded him and he laughed. "Of course. Why else?"

"I thought... Oh, never mind what I thought."

He pulled back a little, still laughing. "Hey, what happened to all that honesty? Or was it just supposed to be me who bared my soul?"

Lynn stepped away. "You're right," she said, not looking at him. "I thought...I thought you might just want me as a live-in baby-sitter."

"Oh." He stopped smiling.

"Mrs. Findley told me about this morning. How the girls were crying and fussing and you—"

"Suddenly decided to get married in order to keep the peace?" His smile was back.

"Well, it—"

"Okay, my timing was a bit off. But I'd been contemplating my future while I shaved. When Allie and Sandy started in on me about dumping you after one night, I suddenly knew the truth. I wanted to be with you always. Not just a night. Not a week or a month or even a year, but the rest of my life. Will you? Marry me?"

Her eyes widened. "Yes, Sam. I will."

The doubts and anxieties that had gripped Lynn dropped away. She pressed against Sam, feeling the strong beat of his heart and the strength of his arms around her. Energy and joy flowed through her, revitalizing her spirit. It was all going to be all right!

Sam released her. "Now," he said. "My turn."

"Huh?" Lynn regarded him, puzzled.

"You told me your fears about me. Now it's my turn to confess to you."

She brushed her hair back from her face. "All right."

"Here are some of my nastier thoughts. I was beginning to think you had set me up, manipulated my emotions and played my daughters like little pianos so you could get your way with Lightning's future."

"What?"

"Hey." He held up both hands. "Don't get mad. I'm just telling you what I was beginning to suspect. And what my partners are convinced you are doing. Not me. Them."

Lynn calmed down. "Oh. I see." She started to pace the length of the Subaru. "This is not good."

"No, it's not." He leaned against the car. "They won't give up without a fight, you know. They need the money too much."

"If only I had it to give them, I'd do it in a minute."

"How about if I do it?"

"What?" She turned and stared at him.

"How about if I buy them out of their half of Lightning. I'll end up owning three-fourths of him, but if you trust me enough to marry me, you ought to trust me with your horse."

"Sam, can you afford it?"

"I don't know yet, for certain, but I do have some money invested in New Orleans real estate. It may take me some time."

"I don't know how much of that we've got."

"We'll come up with something. Especially if we're together."

She smiled. "Sounds good to me."

"You do trust me?"

"I must. I'm going to marry you."

They moved together again, and Sam continued to hold her close without saying another word for some time before they climbed back into the car.

"I'll have to talk to your father soon," Sam said as they drove back toward the city. "I know it's old-fashioned of me, but I want to do this right from now on. I want to ask him for your hand."

"Are you serious? After what he and Tyler did to you?"

"Honey, I've forgiven them, and so should you. They were only looking out for you."

"But I didn't ask them for their help."

"That's beside the point," Sam said. "You should be glad you have people who love you enough to—"

"I know that. But..."

As they drove the rest of the way, they made plans.

"I have a lot of things to learn about kids," she said. "I never would have believed this even a week ago, but I'm kind of relieved that I get to start on older ones.''

"You'll do fine."

"Sam, we'll have to live where I can have my horses. I'll always be involved with them, they are my life, what I do, how I make my living. I won't be able to change that."

"I know that." Sam placed his hand tenderly on her shoulder. "We'll work it out."

They were feeling extremely mellow by the time Sam pulled into his driveway and parked behind her VW. The sun had set, and the soft spring night had settled over the neighborhood. They remained in the car, holding hands for a few minutes.

"They will have heard us drive up," Sam said after a bit. "We should go in."

"Okay." Lynn stretched. "I feel like a cat," she said. "Ready for a nap. So relaxed and content, I could just..."

The side door to the house opened, and Mrs. Findley came out. Her expression indicated that all was not well. Sam hurriedly got out. Lynn followed.

"I prayed you'd be coming back soon," the housekeeper declared. "There's an emergency—"

"The girls?" Sam started inside. Lynn was right behind him.

"No, no." Mrs. Findley held up her hands.

"They're all right. They don't even know there's a problem. No, it's at your place, Lynn. They called."

Lynn raced inside. She grabbed the phone and punched in the ranch number.

No one answered.

She hung up. "Oh, God," she said. "It's Grandpa. I know it." Her emotion was too deep for tears.

Sam came up behind her and put his arms around her. His touch was comforting.

"I don't think so," said Mrs. Findley. "I think it's about your horse, dear." She stood near them, twisting her hands together. "The call came about twenty minutes ago. It was Ruth somebody. She said—"

"Ruth Holden," Lynn said. "She's engaged to my brother, Tyler. Sorry. What did she say?"

"Just that there was an emergency, and you needed to get home as soon as possible."

That was all Lynn needed to hear. She whirled and headed back outside. She got in the VW and thrust the key in the ignition. Sam got in the passenger side. "I'm coming with you," he declared.

"Hang on, then," she warned. She pulled around his Subaru, cutting a hunk of sod out of the side of his lawn, and then Lynn McKinney tore out into the night.

CHAPTER FOURTEEN

LUCK WAS WITH LYNN, and no policeman spotted the blur of the Bug as she drove well above the speed limit out of Austin and onto the highway leading to the ranch. Sam said nothing, allowing her to concentrate on her driving.

"Turn coming up," Lynn warned. She wrenched the wheel. Tires squealed. The Bug rocked.

Sam grabbed for support, bracing himself.

They finally reached the entrance to the ranch and roared down the driveway. When they reached the house, Sam saw half a dozen parked vehicles. The house floodlights were blazing, illuminating the scene.

"Who's here?" he asked.

Lynn gripped the wheel. "Wayne Jackson. Martin Avery. I don't know who else. Sam?" She spoke softly.

"What?"

"I'm scared." She turned to him. "I'm really glad you're here."

"I'm not leaving your side," he promised. He took her hand and squeezed. "We're in this life together now. Remember."

It didn't take long to find the center of action. Down at the stables, quite a crowd was gathered. People were standing in front of the wide doors, but not going inside. Voices rose and fell in talk, punctuated by shouts of anger. As they neared, Lynn saw a pickup with a horse trailer attached, parked right next to the main corral.

"I don't recognize the truck," she said. Her pace increased. Lynn saw J.T., Cynthia, Ruth, Martin and Wayne Jackson. Then, to her great dismay, she spotted Dan and Phil. There were two other men she didn't know. One, obviously some kind of security guard, wore a police uniform, the other a three-piece business suit. "What's going on?" she demanded, walking up to the group. "Who are you people?" she asked the strangers.

"Lynn, honey," her father said, before the newcomers could answer. "They have legal papers to impound Lightning."

"What!" She felt the blood leave her heart and rush to her face. Then she felt Sam's hand on her shoulder. She steadied under his touch and support.

"This is Syms Kellogg," Martin Avery announced, gesturing toward the man in the suit. "He is, laughingly, called a lawyer."

"Thank you, Avery," Kellogg intoned. He was a big man with a smooth, syrupy voice. "I respect you, too. Young lady," he went on, "we have the law on our side, and we have come to take your horse away."

"The hell you will!" Lynn's fists clenched. "Not while I'm breathing, you won't."

"Lynn," Martin said unhappily. "They have a legal document. And the law—"

"The law's been twisted here," Wayne stated. His tanned face was set, masking the anger Lynn knew was simmering in him. Wayne Jackson saw his justice squarely. Not shaped by clever lawyers. "It may be legal, but it isn't right. I don't know how you obtained that paper, but I'm willing to bet some money changed hands under the table!"

"Listen here, Jackson," the other cop said, his tone belligerent. He was a big, beefy man, who regarded the world out of sly little eyes. "You ain't—"

Lynn looked around. "Where's Grandpa?"

Silence fell.

"Where's Grandpa?" she repeated loudly.

"Lynnie?" Hank's voice sounded out of the stable. "Is that you, girl?" Lightning whinnied, drowning out whatever else Hank had yelled.

"Grandpa!" Lynn started for the doorway.

"Oh, no, you don't, missy!" The strange cop grabbed her shoulder, attempting to stop her. His hand was big and heavy, and his grip hurt.

Lynn cried out, flinching. She pulled free.

The cop swore. Tried to grab her again.

And Sam grabbed him, spun him around and swung a fist. It landed with a solid, meaty thunk. The cop stumbled backward. Lynn heard shouts and yelling, but she ran into the stable without looking back. Silently she thanked Sam.

She found Hank on the floor of the stable, positioned right square in front of Lightning's stall. The electric lights were on in the barn, so it was easy enough to see him. The lights, she remembered, were controlled from outside. Hank would be sitting in the dark, otherwise. The old man was sitting on a blanket atop a bale of hay, his ancient, but lethal shotgun resting on his knees. He was contentedly smoking one of his hand-rolled cigarettes.

"Hey, honey," he said, grinning widely. "How you doing?"

"Grandpa!" Lynn knelt beside him, hugging him. "What are you doing? Are you all right? Why do you have the shotgun? And I have told you a thousand, thousand times not to smoke in here."

"Hush up. This one's finished anyway." Hank reached down and extinguished the stub in a coffee can filled with sand. "I ain't gonna start a fire. But

I couldn't sit here for hours, 'less I had my smokes. You know me well enough to understand that.''

"But hours? Why?"

"Ain't nobody else around here that's got the guts to defend your stupid nag," Hank declared. "I told 'em anybody stuck their head in here, I'd blow it off. Friend or enemy. That's kept 'em out and thinkin'.'' He grinned. "I let you in, 'course."

"Grandpa." Lynn sank down to sit on her rear. "You hate this horse. Why are you doing this?"

"Don't hate you, though, Sugar. That's why." Hank fumbled for another cigarette. He had several in his shirt pocket. Apparently he'd taken time to roll a fresh bunch before setting himself up for a siege. But his hand was trembling too much for him to get a grip.

Lynn leaned over, took a cigarette from his pocket and handed it to him. She lit it for him, and Hank gratefully sucked in smoke. Above them, Lightning stuck his head out of his stall and whickered at Lynn, hopefully. She reached up and patted his nose. Emotions almost too strong to bear filled her, but she kept her expression calm, her eyes dry and her voice steady. "I really, really love you, Grandpa," she said. "Thanks."

"I know you do, and it's all right. You're welcome." He drew in more smoke. "How'd you get past them bastards, anyways?"

"Sam." She stood and scratched gently around Lightning's ears. "He decked the cop when he tried to stop me. Not Wayne. The other one."

"Shoot!" Hank laughed and slapped his leg. "Hot damn! Knew that boy was gonna turn out to be some use. Heh, heh. Guess he'll go to jail, too, now," he added, clearly relishing the prospect. "Think they might put us in the same cell? I could still use a good dentist."

"Maybe, Grandpa." Lynn gave her horse an affectionate slap on the neck and sat back down. "You want me to hold that shotgun for a while? Aren't you kind of tired?"

Hank glared at her. "Hell, no. Think I'm some fool? I give you this gun, you'd be the one goin' to jail. No, girlie. This here is man's work."

Lynn leaned back against the stall door. No point in arguing with Hank Travis. "Okay. Just asking."

"Lynn!" It was Martin Avery. "Can you talk to us?"

"Sure," she called back. "What do you want?"

"Don't talk to that goddamn, slimy lawyer," Hank warned. "He's just as bad as the others, sayin' the papers is legal. Supposed to be your Daddy's friend. Ha! Some kind of friend."

"Lynn?" This time it was J.T. "Can you get him to come out?"

"No!" yelled Hank. "She cain't. But it ain't her fault. I got the gun."

"He's all right, Daddy," Lynn replied, knowing that his grandfather's welfare was her father's main concern. "He's fine, and so am I."

There was no immediate reply. Then she heard the sound of several more vehicles pulling up outside the stables. She put her hand on Hank's arm and tensed. But no one tried to come inside.

Instead, voices were raised in anger again, and there was the sound of another scuffle.

"Lynn," Sam hollered. "They're arresting me, but don't worry about it. I love you!"

Now, she stood. "Sam!" Her voice broke. "Oh, God, Grandpa. What can I do! I can't let him go to jail for me!"

"Sure, you can. Let the boy do it. He wants to. Shows he's got sand." Hank put out his cigarette. "You wanta give up this nag?" he asked, squinting up at her.

"No. But Sam is—"

"Sam's gonna be right pissed if you give up when he's done somethin' like gettin' hisself arrested for you." Hank spit into a corner. "He has sacrificed for his love, Lynnie. You don't let a man down who's done that."

She sat back on the floor. "You're right. And if I really should give us up, Daddy would be telling me to, wouldn't he?"

"Damn right, he would." Hank grinned, agreeing. "He's a fighter, especially when it comes to you children. So, you sit tight, you hear."

That started another train of thought in Lynn's mind. Why hadn't her father insisted she come out, bringing Hank with her? He probably knew she could get him to come out, if she tried. But J.T. had remained uncharacteristically silent. Actually, so had everyone else, including Ruth, who had made the phone call, and Cynthia, who...

And Tyler...

Where was Tyler?

Hank took out another cigarette. His hand wasn't shaking so badly now. "Fire me up, again, will you?"

Lynn lit it for him. And they sat together while the old man blew smoke rings up at the racehorse's nose. Oddly, Lightning didn't seem to mind.

Things seemed quiet for a while. Murmurs of anxious conversation came from the group outside, but no more yelling or sounds of violence. Lynn tried to relax.

Finally, Hank said, "You trust me, honey?"

"Sure, Grandpa. I always have." She patted his shoulder.

"Then, just wait with me, here. I ain't sittin' tight for my health. I got things agoin' on. Just don't want to talk about 'em, yet. Some snake out there might be listenin' in."

"I see." Lynn regarded her great-grandfather. He'd outsmarted scores of men in his day, she knew. Just because he was as ancient as the land and somedays as feeble as a baby was no reason to doubt him when he had his stuff together.

As he seemed to have right now.

"Wait with me, Lynnie," he said. "And don't ask no questions."

"Okay," she said. "I hear and obey. No questions asked."

Hank chuckled. "Damn. Wish I could get that down in writin'. Or on one of them fancy tape recorders. No livin' man's gonna believe me when I tell him you said that." He chuckled some more.

Lynn laughed, too, and punched the old man playfully in the arm. Then she settled down for a long wait.

Hours passed. Lynn nodded off to sleep several times, but jerked awake after a few minutes of dozing. The least she could do for Hank was keep him company.

"I'd kill for some coffee," she muttered.

"Have a smoke," Hank said.

"No, thanks." Lynn leaned back against the stall. Inside, she heard Lightning shift position, heavily.

"Boy gonna marry you?" Hank asked suddenly. "He pop the question yet?"

"Uh, yes. Actually, just a few hours ago. Out at a rest stop on the highway."

Hank snorted. "Not real romantic, is he?"

"Sam loves me. That's all that matters."

"Kids know?"

"Yes. They're happy."

Hank cleared his throat. "You. A stepmama. Hum. Don't seem possible or right, somehow."

Lynn had to smile. "Not to me, either, when I think about it, cold. But I can't help it. I fell in love with a man with two kids. I have no choice."

"Lucky devil." Hank spit. "Him, I mean. Not you."

"I know."

More time passed. Lynn did not sleep again.

"You gonna have a kid of your own?" Hank asked. His voice sounded old now. Not firm, as it had been earlier.

Lynn looked at him carefully. "Yes," she said. "I surely plan to."

He smiled. "Good." He moved the shotgun. "That's a comfort to my soul."

Lynn was about to reply when she heard renewed commotion from outside. In the stall behind her, she heard Lightning moving. Then, the horse let out a shrill, challenging whinny and kicked at the stall wall.

Lynn stood. "What's going on? What is it?"

Hank struggled to his feet, the shotgun steady in his hands. "Damned if I know. Can't hear as well as I used to." He glanced around. "Get yourself up in the loft, and see what you can see."

Lynn obeyed. The loft had an opening that overlooked the yard below. She'd be able to see without being seen.

She scurried up the ladder and across the hay-strewn upper floor to the gate at the end. Opening it slightly, she looked down. Fear gripped her.

The ranch hands, who had not been around when she and Sam arrived, were now out there in force. Circling the strange lawmen—there were now five of them—they looked grim and determined. Lynn saw no guns, but she did catch a glimpse of a clenched fist here and there and at least one knife in a belt sheath. She'd never thought of her father's employees as dangerous before. Tonight, they looked like men who were ready to fight fiercely for their boss.

The encircled lawmen looked nervous. Wayne was talking to them, but they were watching the cowboys, not listening to the sheriff. Martin was pacing anxiously at the perimeter. The dentists and their lawyer were back beside the pickup and trailer. Her father and Ken were in deep discussion. J.T.'s face in the glaring floodlight was drawn and weary. The women were gone. Tyler was still nowhere to be seen.

Lynn drew back. While she was willing to accept the consequence of her own actions and even to allow Sam to help her, even to let Sam suffer, as he had chosen, she was not willing to let others put themselves at risk just out of loyalty to her father and the ranch. She had to act.

She hurried back across the loft floor and shinned down the narrow ladder. Hank came over. "What's up?"

"The boys are out there," she explained, going into the tack room and taking out a bridle. "If I don't stop them, they're likely to make a whole lot of trouble."

"Your daddy can handle them."

"Daddy looks exhausted." Lynn went back to Lightning's stall. At the sound of jingling tack, the stallion whinnied again and stuck his head out of the door. "I can't let this go on any longer."

Hank was silent. Then, "All right. You have to do what you have to do," he said. He broke the shotgun and unloaded it. "Tell 'em I'll give myself up peaceful."

"I won't let them take you to jail, Grandpa." Lynn went into the stall and started putting the bridle on

Lightning. "I'll do something. I'll think of something."

"Is it gettin' light yet?" Hank's voice was thin and tired sounding. "Sun comin' up?"

"I don't know. I didn't see. I think so, but I was too busy looking at the people to notice for sure." She opened the stall door and led the eager Lightning out. "Why?"

"No reason. I think it's near dawn, anyways. If it ain't, promise you'll delay doin' anythin' drastic till that sun's right up." Hank sank back down to sit on the floor. He patted his shirt pocket. "Damn. I'm outa smokes. Send some fixin's to me at the jail, will you?"

"You aren't going to jail, Grandpa." She leaned over and kissed his cheek. "I'll make sure of that," she added.

Then she mounted Lightning bareback.

"Go show 'em, Lynnie," Hank said. "Show 'em what you're made of! And remember what I said. Wait for the sun, child."

"I will, Grandpa," she said, sitting straight and proud. She spoke to her horse, and Lightning moved.

She rode out into the dawn, the horse's hooves striking the wooden floor of the stable like muffled drumbeats announcing her arrival to those outside.

All conversation, argument and talk ceased as she came into view. Everyone stared at her.

The floodlights were still on, but they shone pale and weak as the sky to the east pearled up with a peach glow. No sun yet, but the day was coming. The human faces looked wan and weary. Skin stretched by tension, eyes reddened by anger and fear.

Lightning shied as he spotted the crowd of people, but she calmed him with a touch and a murmur. He then tried to turn toward the path leading down to the racetrack, intent on following their normal routine, even if his beloved rider had chosen not to saddle him up this morning.

"No, boy," Lynn said. "Not today." She reined him to a halt, and he stood under her, trembling with eagerness to run and frustration at being held back. She felt his every nerve as if it were connected to hers.

All watched her. No one said a word.

"I don't want anyone hurt," she said. "I give up. I'll make a deal. Let Grandpa go on back to his house to bed. He's real tired. And then I'll talk to you people about Lightning."

"The time for talk is past! Young woman, you're in serious trouble," Syms Kellogg said, striding forward. "I intend to see that criminal charges are—"

"Shut the hell up, Kellogg," J.T. said, moving over to his daughter's side. Lightning tolerated his nearness, knowing him, but his skin quivered nervously beneath Lynn's legs. "Nothing criminal's been done here tonight. And thanks to Lynn, nothing will be."

"Her lover's been arrested for assaulting an officer," the heavyset lawyer declared, coming closer. He put his finger near J.T.'s face, stabbing at the air to emphasize his point. "She's blocked the implementation of a legal order. We can get her for obstruction, as well."

"Try it," said Martin Avery. "And I can guarantee all of you scum a lawsuit for false arrest. In fact, I'm considering it in Russell's case as well. Your rent-a-cop was trying to rough up Miss McKinney when Sam stopped him. It seems to me it was more a defensive act than aggression on the part of a citizen. Your cop was real quick to hit back, and he has no direct jurisdiction out here. Only Wayne Jackson can officially arrest anyone in this county unless it's a federal case, and your boy is hardly FBI material."

Lynn blinked. She hadn't considered this. "Then did Wayne arrest Sam? Wayne, did you?"

Wayne Jackson looked embarrassed. "I didn't really arrest him, just got him out of the way. For his own good, Lynn. He was pretty hot. Ready to tear into the guy. I've seen him like that before, you remember. He wasn't exactly being reasonable about the whole thing, so I decided to let him cool off over in the squad car." He pointed up toward the house.

"Oh." Lightning shifted sideways. Lynn calmed him down. "Then he's not in jail?"

"Not yet."

Lynn turned to her father. "Daddy, I—"

Whatever Lynn was about to say was lost. Just as she spoke, Syms Kellogg reached for Lightning's bridle.

A mistake. As the big beefy hand tried to grab, Lightning flattened his ears, pulled back his lips and bit. His strong teeth gripped the lawyer's hand, chomping down with an energy fueled by a night of disturbances and a dawn of frustrated expectations. Kellogg screamed like a steam whistle, and Lightning let go. He trumpeted a wild whinny, echoing Kellogg's scream, and reared up, taking Lynn entirely by surprise. His neck and withers struck her chest, knocking the breath from her and stunning her for a second. She lost her hold on the reins, but instinctively grabbed his thick mane.

And Lightning took off.

He ran through the crowd, which had already parted for him. He thundered up the path toward the ranch house, his long legs eating up the distance in a moment. Lynn recovered, but didn't try for the reins yet. If he jumped an obstruction while she was groping for the leather, she would be dumped for certain. Until they were on a long, clear stretch, she knew her best hope was just to cling to his back like a burr.

Her best hope, and his.

They tore past the front yard and the house. Out of the corner of her eye, she saw the police cruiser with Sam in the back seat. The front door of the house opened, and Ruth and Cynthia ran out, their faces white and their mouths round with horror. Lightning's hooves clattered on the stone walk as he raced around the house. From the kitchen door, she saw Virginia and Lettie Mae emerge. Heard shouts and screams. Then she was past them all. The hooves clunked on the concrete around the empty swimming pool.

The rose garden loomed ahead. Fence and all. Lynn clung. Lightning was a racehorse, not a jumper. She prayed that he would clear the rail fence and not hurt himself. She braced...

And had the breath knocked out of her once more when Lightning came to a dead stop, mere inches from the fence.

"Oooof!" She gasped and groped for the reins. She was too far up on his neck. The reins were behind her. Lightning turned and started to trot along the fence line. Lynn slid back, trying to regain a solid seat, but the gait threw her to one side, then the other. She held on only by her hands in his mane. "Whoa! Dammit!" she yelled.

And Lightning stopped.

"Oh!" She leaned forward, breathing hard. The reins seemed to slide right into her hands. "Oh," she repeated softly.

"Lynn!" Virginia came on a dead run, Lettie Mae right behind her. Ruth and Cynthia were only yards behind them. All four women looked terrified.

"Are you all right, child?" Lettie Mae passed Virginia and reached the fence first. "Are you hurt?"

Lynn slid off Lightning, keeping a firm hold on the reins. "I'm fine," she said. "That obnoxious lawyer tried to grab him and Lightning bit him."

"But he was running away with you," Cynthia said, breathing hard. "I saw—"

"You saw Lightning running," Lynn said. "But not away. I just let him go until I could get control again without risking any harm." She patted her horse's cheek. "Good boy. He stopped at the right place. Right at the roses."

Lightning whoofed. He seemed extremely pleased with himself.

"Is that like a true winner, or what?" Lynn cooed, stroking his velvety nose.

Ruth laughed, the sound full of relief. "I should have known you'd be all right," she said. "I've never seen a centaur before today. You and the horse looked like one being."

"Honey, you are closer to the truth than you know," declared Lettie Mae, her expression wry, but proud.

"Lynn! Lynn!"

Sam's shout made her turn away from the horse. Lynn saw him coming around the side of the house. His hands were behind him, and there was some blood on his clothes. He had a bruise over his eye that was purpling as well. She handed the reins to Cynthia and ran to him. They met at the swimming pool and she put her arms around him.

"I thought..." They both spoke the words at the same time. Lynn saw that he was handcuffed.

"How in the world did you get loose, Sam?" she cried. "You're cut!"

"I kicked out the window," he said, grinning at her. "Scratched myself up a bit, climbing out, but I had to get to you. Amazing what adrenaline can do when the blood's up." He stopped smiling. "Are you all right? Who stopped the runaway?"

Lynn pointed. "Himself." Lightning was happily receiving the attention of the four women. Reveling in it, Lynn decided, watching him. "He saw the fence and stopped. He really wasn't bolting. Just letting off steam. He was just nervous and startled. I... Sam, you're the one who's hurt. You're bleeding!"

She didn't get to say the rest. Sam, his hands pinned behind him, bent his head and kissed her.

The world and all its problems disappeared.

They came back almost immediately. The sound of men shouting alerted them to reality. "They're coming," Sam said. "We've got to do something. But what?"

"This." Lynn grabbed his arm and led him over to the horse and the other women. "Virginia, get him inside and take care of his wounds. Ruth, can you hacksaw off those cuffs?"

"I think so," Ruth said, eyeing the plastic cuffs speculatively. "Thank goodness they aren't the old metal kind."

"What about Lightning?" Sam asked. "What are you going to do? Just give him up?"

Lynn shook her head. "I was when I thought I had to in order to avoid violence. But now I'm not. Not yet, anyway. Grandpa was trying to tell me something back in the stable. Something is going on that none of us know about." She looked at Ruth. "Where's Tyler?"

Ruth shrugged, the gesture stiff with concern. "I don't know. I'm worried, too. But he took off shortly after that crowd arrived. It's been a long time."

"I think he's gone for the cavalry, so to speak," Cynthia offered. "But J.T. wouldn't say anything to me, either. I expect they don't want us womenfolk to get our hopes up," she added, a little sarcastically.

"That's the McKinney male way," Virginia informed her.

"Indeed it is." Lettie Mae patted Lightning. "I never knew this animal was so nice. Think he'd like some sugar or an apple or something?"

"Don't you dare! Give him a carrot, if you want to treat him." Lynn reached for the reins. "Get Sam inside. I'm putting Big Boy here in the rose garden."

"What?" They all stared.

"Uh-huh." Lynn opened the gate and led him in. Then she slipped the bridle off. Lightning stomped in pleasure, tossed his inky mane, then trotted off to investigate his new enclosure.

"I bet even money no one will have the guts to come in here after him," she said, coming out and closing the gate. "Not only will they have a 'wild and crazy,' half-ton stallion to contend with, but who wants to fight thorns in the process? Lightning's hair coat will protect him, but humans have thin skin."

Nobody argued with her.

"Lightning's fine. I'm fine. Now," she said, "let's worry about Sam."

CHAPTER FIFTEEN

WHEN J.T. SAW the big black Thoroughbred browsing contentedly in the rose garden, he breathed a long sigh of great relief. He hadn't really believed Lynn was in danger, knowing that she rode better than she walked, but it was still frightening to see her tear off. "She's inside," he told Wayne and Martin. "Probably having her morning coffee and laughing at all of us."

"Think Russell's in there, too?" Wayne was not happy. "The son of a bitch kicked out my squad car window. I can't believe he managed that."

"He saw his woman in danger," Hank said. "Musta given him the strength. Proves he's a real man."

"Proves he's stupid," said Martin. "I might be able to get him out of the assault charge, but deliberately destroying county property is another matter entirely."

"How long do you figure Ken and the boys can keep them city rattlers shut up in their pickup?" Hank asked J.T., ignoring Martin and the sheriff.

"When's Tyler gonna get his ass back here, anyways? I got real damn tired out in that stable."

"I know, Hank." J.T. put his arm around the old man's shoulders. "Why don't you go take a nap until—"

"Like hell. I ain't sleepin' until I know my Lynnie and her damn nag are safe."

"Well, you just might find out in a few minutes." Wayne pointed at the plume of dust in the distance. Someone was driving down the road at a fast clip. "Let's go see."

The four men walked back around the side of the house to the front. Tyler slid the pickup to a stop. He left the engine running and jumped out, a briefcase in his left hand.

"I got it!" he yelled, taking out a piece of paper. "You were right, Grandpa. Your old friend, the judge, came through. Where's the other lawyer?"

"You got what?" Lynn stood at the opened front door. Sam appeared by her side. "A piece of paper. Will that save Lightning for me, Tyler?"

Tyler looked up at his little sister. And her future husband. "I can promise it will help. And will you two forgive me?"

Sam put his hands on Lynn's shoulders. "We will."

"What happened to you?" Tyler asked, staring.

"Run in with a cop car," Sam said.

"You got a nerve, Russell," Wayne Jackson said angrily. "Standing there like you—"

"Oh, hush the hell up, Wayne." Hank walked over to Tyler. His posture was erect, and he looked decades younger than his ninety-nine years. "You got the court order, son?"

"I did, Grandpa. You were right. That judge did remember you. I very nearly didn't get the order because of *what* he remembered, but apparently the association you two had about thirty years ago was such that he's willing to—"

"Never mind that." Hank waved a hand. "Just take them papers down to the shark in the truck. Once he sees 'em, he'll leave Lynnie alone."

"What have you done?" Sam came out of the doorway and down the stairs. He was limping slightly and several bandages showed on his arms and face. The skin around one eye was turning dark purple. "You didn't buy the horse, did you?"

Tyler shook his head. "No. Wish I could have. I just got a stay of that impound order. The judge who issued it for Syms Kellogg and his two clients was bribed. Under some pressure, he privately admitted it, though I doubt we could get him to confess publicly."

"Then, how...?"

"The other judge Grandpa and Daddy sent me to is honest, and willing to get out of bed in the middle of the night to listen to anyone related to Hank Travis.''

Tyler paused and eyed his great-grandfather. ''Seems he and Grandpa were in some kind of card game together years ago, and he lost a considerable amount of cash and Grandpa bailed him out....'' He stopped when Hank growled a warning at him. Then he looked up at Lynn again. ''You're still in the soup, I'm afraid. This is only to give you some time to figure out some other way to get control of Lightning.''

''We already have a few ideas,'' Lynn said. She linked arms with Sam. ''We've been talking.''

''First things first, Lynn.'' Sam touched her face tenderly, then turned to J.T. McKinney and said, ''Sir, I'd like to marry your daughter. Do we have your blessing?''

J.T. scowled, then grinned widely. ''Since I guess you wouldn't ask me if you hadn't asked her first, I figure I'd better say yes. Because I sure as hell don't want to have to be the one to go into that briar patch after her horse! Yes, I give you both my blessings, and then some!''

Lynn ran down the steps and joyously threw herself at the men of her family. Tyler, her daddy, her great-granddaddy.

And then she ran back up the steps and embraced Samuel Russell, D.D.S.

ALMOST A MONTH LATER, Lynn and Sam sat in Whit Bailey's den. Lynn had her briefcase open, and legal papers and documents were spilled all over the coffee table. The professor had been studying some of them. His silence had caused Lynn's anxiety level to rise to the point where she wanted to scream, but she kept silent.

And prayed.

"Hmm. Invest in your horse?" Whit Bailey said finally. "Why, I suppose I might consider it." He humphed and cleared his throat. "Horse racing. Though it's called the sport of kings, it's not exactly the sort of thing one finds a professor of music doing, is it?"

"It's a gamble," Lynn admitted. "But a good one. As you can see from the investment proposal."

"Ah, yes." Whit adjusted his glasses. "If the horse wins, and if he breeds true, and if... My dear, aren't there quite a few 'ifs' involved here?"

Lynn gritted her teeth. Whit Bailey sounded like her father! "Yes. I agree. But some risks are worth taking. Think about Sandy. Isn't she just as much of a gamble for you? For anyone who helps and encourages her and teaches her, hoping she will go on with her musical talent and make a career worth the investment of time and energy."

Whit removed his glasses. He gazed at Sam. "Good luck, my boy. You're absolutely sure you wish to marry this woman?"

Sam smiled. "I am."

Whit shook his head. "I pity you when you get into a disagreement with her. You are doomed to defeat."

"I've already discovered that," Sam replied, his tone and expression indicating he was happy with the find.

"Well." Whit returned his glasses to his face. "What of the two investors whose part I would be buying out? Have they no objections to selling, given the extremely optimistic forecast, dollar-wise?"

"They are in deep legal and financial quicksand," Sam said. "They've overspent on a clinic building and have done some creative accounting, trying to make ends meet. Now they've been audited and they were hoping to recoup some instant cash from Lightning and have it on hand to make a deal with the IRS when push came to shove."

"And that didn't happen? The cash, I mean."

"It didn't happen because I refused to race Lightning with a view to selling him, which was their intent," Lynn explained. "They were planning on having him make a small, but impressive splash in some local and regional runs, then to enter him in a contest where the winning horses are open to any buyer willing to pay the price. If they had their way, Lightning would be sold to strangers by the end of the summer." She paused. "I would have taken him out of racing before I let that happen."

"And so you did, it seems. He hasn't raced in some time, according to your records." Whit studied her. "Are you now so certain he'll be able to get back...what would you say, into the saddle? Into the swim?"

"I am certain," she replied. "Absolutely certain."

"He's racing for the first time again this Sunday over in Louisiana against some tough competition," Sam said. "If you're still not sure, why don't you come and watch him. We're all going, and you're more than welcome to ride along. I can guarantee once you see him in action, you'll be convinced."

Whit took off his glasses again. "I'll be there," he said. "But, my young friends, I'm already convinced. I already told you, Lynn, that I wanted to do something for you since you helped so much with Alexandra. This is but a small matter, compared to the child. I will write you a check for one half share in your Lightning. And I promise that as long as you keep out of my professional management of Alexandra Russell, I will keep out of your professional management of Lightning."

Lynn struggled to keep from jumping up and shouting for joy. She held out her hand. "Deal," she said. "You have a deal!"

LYNN AND SAM pulled up in front of Dr. Purdy's clinic, where Sam had set up his temporary office. He had been ordered to offer one hundred hours of community service and to pay for repairs to Wayne's car. Sam had suggested a free dental clinic in Crystal Creek and the judge had agreed. Although the clinic wasn't completely supplied with proper dentistry gear, Sam had brought out a load of equipment from his office in Austin, and he was able to provide adequate first-line care for the people who came for the free treatment.

Hank Travis was his first patient.

"Your great-grandfather was in yesterday afternoon again," Sam told her as Lynn turned off the engine. "I haven't figured out if he hangs out with me because he enjoys my company or if he gets a sadistic kick out of goading my patients before I see them."

"He's having a ball," Lynn replied. "He likes you."

"*Now,* he does. If I hadn't gotten engaged to you, I doubt I'd still be wearing my head."

"That's probably true, too. Grandpa tends to be kind of old-fashioned."

Sam reached to touch her hand. "Let's name our first male child after him."

Lynn felt a lump form in her throat. "Okay by me. I...I just..."

"What, honey? Remember, no secrets anymore."

"It's nothing," Lynn said, not meeting his eyes. "I'm just glad all the problems are solved. I guess I'm kind of coming down."

"Are you worried about Sunday?" He studied her intently.

"No." She flashed a smile. "Piece of cake."

"Sure?"

"Yep."

"Liar." He kissed her again. "You are worried, aren't you?"

Lynn threw her arms around his neck and clung to him. "I'm not worried," she whispered. "I'm terrified. The Creole Stakes is big-time, tough competition. What if my judgment is off? What if he's not ready yet? What if I ruined him? What if I've been all wrong?"

Sam held her tight. "You haven't. I believe in you."

AFTER RISING EARLY Sunday morning, Lynn found she couldn't eat. The tension in her was almost out of control. Her body rejected the idea of food, even though she knew she ought to force something down.

Lettie Mae finally got her to choke a "health shake" past her nervous throat. She worried about everything—herself, Sam, Whit Bailey, her family, the girls and, of course, at the top of the list, Lightning.

Lightning had been stabled over at the Louisiana track for several days in an effort to get him settled down after traveling. Every morning for days, Tyler had flown her over in the ranch plane so she could work with the horse. But Lightning was still not right. His patience was at an all-time low, and he tended to want to fight the other horses, not run with them. She was terrified that all the excitement and disruption of the past weeks would take their toll on him, and his energy level would not be up to par for the real thing.

But now there was nothing more to do. Only hope, pray and do the very best job of riding she'd ever done in her entire life.

Tyler flew her over as usual and returned to join the rest of the family for the cavalcade from Crystal Creek. It was a large group of cars, an even larger group of folks, and the level of accumulated excitement and tension was unmeasurable.

Sam was so jumpy, he was sure his skin was going to crawl right off his body. Only the presence of his children kept him sane. They were having fun and didn't seem worried at all.

Just happy. Sam decided he would do well to take lessons on that from them.

Hours later Lynn McKinney rode her horse toward the metal starting gates and her fear started to fade. The earthy smell of the track, the sweet-acrid scent of the horses, the exciting sound of the cheering crowd and the clomp-clomp-clomp of hooves on the dirt, the smooth feel of the silks against her skin, the itch of nervous sweat on her face and the tightness of the hat on her head all brought back reality.

She rode a true champion. That was the reality.

She spotted her family and her family-to-be in the stands, but she didn't wave. Much as she wanted to, it would not be professional.

Sam watched her from the box that J.T. had rented. He was so proud of her, so in love with her, so...

So scared for her. She looked so tiny out there with the rest of the riders—all men—and the huge horses. If Lightning should stumble...

But he was going to have to get used to the danger, he reminded himself. The danger, the love and the glory. They went together, after all. He felt his stomach knot in alarm and his heart jump to his throat as he saw Lightning prance violently in place suddenly, apparently trying to break from Lynn's control.

"Daddy," Allie asked, "is she all right?"

"Sure, she is," Sandy said.

Hank spoke. "That's right, young'n. Don't nobody have to worry. He's just eager to beat the pants off the world. She's got him where she wants him. Believe me. Don't you doubt it, son."

Sam muttered thanks for the reassurance.

Lynn held Lightning to her with a firm grip on his reins. The big colt seemed to understand now what was happening. Lynn could sense that he wanted, with all of his great heart, to burst forth from the gate and destroy the track with his speed. She murmured patience to him, asking him to trust her.

Lightning heard her and settled. He whoofed in frustration and stomped, but resumed his place at the starting gate. His skin and muscles quivered restlessly and his ears twitched, but otherwise he did not move.

He was waiting.

And Sam was watching, his fears not allayed one bit by Hank's words or his daughter's confidence. That woman on that enormous horse was his love, and she was risking herself! Allie understood. She reached for and held her father's hand, and he could feel the tension in her.

And then, suddenly the race was on, and he found his fear vanishing in the excitement that brought him to his feet with a roar. Beside him, Hank yelled for all he was worth and J.T.'s bellow nearly drowned out the loudspeaker. Allie and Sandy were screaming and jumping up and down. The entire McKinney clan—Tyler, Ruth, Cal, Serena, Cynthia, Lettie Mae, Virginia, Beverly—were yelling for their favorite.

The eight horses in the race thundered out of the starting gate and down the track. They all moved fast, but to Sam's surprise and dismay, three of them were ahead of Lightning. A bay, another black and a sorrel, were trouncing the rest of the field. Sam yelled for Lynn to get going!

But she didn't. Lightning, much bigger than any of the other contenders, just plodded along. He looked as if he was struggling to keep pace. From Sam's position up in the stands, the damn horse just seemed to be taking a walk! He yelled some more. "Go! Go! Go!"

"Move it!" J.T. screamed, raising both arms in the air.

"Go, Lynnie!" screeched Hank Travis.

Sam and his daughters chorused encouragement. Sam began to be afraid again. If she lost, what would happen? Her heart, her spirit would be broken! And their future would be in peril. He glanced over at Whit Bailey.

Whit looked very concerned. Cal McKinney leaned over and whispered something to the professor. And then Whit smiled.

Sam wished he knew what Cal had shared. He closed his eyes for a second.

"Daddy! Look!" Allie grabbed at his arm.

"She's doing it!" Sandy yodeled. "Look at them!"

Sam did. Lightning was still running a slow fourth.

Then, something happened.

Out on the track, Lynn knew it was time. She leaned even farther over her horse and whispered. "Now, fella. Go for it, now!" She felt him wait for an instant, gathering his energies and focusing his strength.

Lightning galvanized. The incredible power and discipline always resident in his heart and muscles poured out, and he began to run as he had not been doing before. He ran, and the wind whistled and shrieked past Lynn's face and in her ears. Out of the corner of her eye, she saw the sorrel as they passed.

Then, the other black.

And, finally, the bay in the lead. The track ahead was clear. Lightning flew for the finish.

They ran faster than the wind, faster than sound, faster than light itself. Faster, even, than time.

It was the race of their lives.

Beneath her, beneath the narrow, thin racing saddle, she felt the powerful muscles as Lightning ran. Part of her, but also apart. She merged her strength with his strength and gave him her will and her skill to win, to match his own drive to victory.

They were a team. Unbeatable, unique and far more than just the sum of the two of them, woman and horse. Together, they were a champion, a winner, a force that could not be defeated. They ran to where the finish line waited. No brick walls or stumbling anymore!

Up in the stands, Sam could see that she had always been in charge of the race. No horse had gotten ahead of her without her permission. She could have let her big black beast take the lead from the very beginning, but she had chosen to wait for the dramatic moment to pull out the stops. Watching her race to win, he knew no matter what the future held, he was bound by love and faith to Lynn and her dreams. They were his dreams, too.

He cheered until he went hoarse.

And Lynn on Lightning blew the rest of the field away.

Before the official awarding of the prize, Sam left the stands and found a telephone. He made one call, confirming something he'd already planned. Then he returned to the stands.

Sam waited until everyone else had tendered their congratulations. Then, he walked into the winner's circle and took his love in his arms. He reached down and took off her riding cap, smoothed her sweaty hair, kissed her smiling lips and said, ''I think roses are in order for the winner.''

And from out of the stands came a parade of florist delivery folk, each one carrying bundles of roses.

If you enjoyed
WHITE LIGHTNING

don't miss
*EVEN THE NIGHTS
ARE BETTER*
by Margot Dalton

the fifth installment of the
Crystal Creek series
coming to you in July

Vernon Trent has loved Carolyn Townsend ever since they were in the first grade. But he never told her, and by the time he came back from Vietnam, she was married.

Now, twenty years later, the widowed Carolyn can sense there is something Vern wants to share with her. Suddenly she isn't sure she wants to hear what her childhood friend has to say. It could change things between them forever.

Watch for it next month, wherever Harlequin books are sold.

**If you enjoyed WHITE LIGHTNING,
you'll love**

Superromance #557
THE MARRIAGE TICKET
by Sharon Brondos

Raising twin children on her own isn't easy. Allison Ford
has learned to rely on her own judgment and stand up for
what she believes. Which is why she is the perfect person
to help Matt Glass prove that he can be a father to his
recently orphaned niece—and thwart scheming relatives
who want to take his sister's baby away.

THE MARRIAGE TICKET

This poignant, sometimes humorous, always involving
Superromance novel is part of the exciting WOMEN WHO
DARE! series. These books feature unique heroines who
know their own minds and will dare anything for love.

**THE MARRIAGE TICKET by Sharon Brondos will be
available next month wherever Superromance books are sold.**

SBCC1

New York Times Bestselling Author

Sandra Brown

Tomorrow's Promise

**She cherished the memory
of love but was consumed
by a new passion too
fierce to ignore.**

For Keely Preston, the memory of her husband
Mark has been frozen in time since the day he was
listed as missing in action. And now, twelve years
later, twenty-six men listed as MIA have been
found.

Keely's torn between hope for Mark and despair
for herself. Because now, after all the years of
waiting, she has met another man!

**Don't miss TOMORROW'S PROMISE by
SANDRA BROWN.**

**Available in June wherever Harlequin
books are sold.**

TP

**Relive the romance...
Harlequin and Silhouette
are proud to present**

by Request

A program of collections of three complete novels by the most requested authors with the most requested themes. Be sure to look for one volume each month with three complete novels by top name authors.

In June: **NINE MONTHS** Penny Jordan
Stella Cameron
Janice Kaiser

Three women pregnant and alone. But a lot can happen in nine months!

In July: **DADDY'S
HOME** Kristin James
Naomi Horton
Mary Lynn Baxter

Daddy's Home... and his presence is long overdue!

In August: **FORGOTTEN
PAST** Barbara Kaye
Pamela Browning
Nancy Martin

Do you dare to create a future if you've forgotten the past?

Available at your favorite retail outlet.

HARLEQUIN® *Silhouette*

REQ-G

BE PART OF CRYSTAL CREEK
WITH THIS FABULOUS FREE GIFT!

The attractive Crystal Creek cowboy boot brooch—beautifully crafted and finished in a lovely silver tone—is the perfect accessory to any outfit!

As you share the passions and influence of the people of Crystal Creek ... and experience the excitement of hot Texas nights, smooth Texas charm and dangerously sexy cowboys—you need to collect only three proofs-of-purchase for the Crystal Creek cowboy boot brooch to become YOURS ... *ABSOLUTELY FREE!*

HOW TO CLAIM YOUR ATTRACTIVE CRYSTAL CREEK COWBOY BOOT BROOCH... To receive your free gift, complete the Collector Card—located in the insert in this book—according to the directions on it. If you prefer not to use the Collector Card, or if it is missing, when you've collected three Proofs from three books, write your name and address on a blank piece of paper, place in an envelope with $1.95 (Postage and Handling) and mail to:

IN THE U.S.A.:
HARLEQUIN CRYSTAL CREEK PROMOTION
P.O. BOX 9071
BUFFALO, NY 14269-9071

IN CANADA:
HARLEQUIN CRYSTAL CREEK PROMOTION
P.O. BOX 604
FORT ERIE, ONTARIO L2A 5X3

Below you'll find a proof-of-purchase. You'll find one in the back pages of every Crystal Creek novel ... every month!

PREMIUM OFFER TERMS

Requests must be received no later than March 31, 1994. Only original proofs of purchase accepted. Limit: (1) one gift per name, family, group, organization. Cowboy boot brooch may differ slightly from photo. Please allow 6 to 8 weeks for receipt of gift. Offer good while quantities of gifts last. In the event an ordered gift is no longer available, you will receive a free, previously unpublished Harlequin book for every proof-of-purchase you have submitted with your request plus a refund of the postage and handling charge you have included. Offer good in the U.S.A. and Canada only.

Here's a proof of purchase—start collecting today!

ONE
PROOF-OF-PURCHASE

Crystal Creek

088-KAW

CCPOPR